**"I don't want to go, Emily, but if that's what you want, I will."**

She looked up, met his cloudy gaze, and opened her mouth to answer him—to tell him that, yes, she wanted him to go away, never to bother her again, to leave Children's and never to purposely cross her path again. She *did* want all those things.

But none of that came out, and whatever she'd been going to say was lost to the pressure of Lucas's mouth covering hers in a kiss.

Dear Reader,

Sometimes a story idea hits and just takes off. Emily and Lucas's story was that way. Occasionally couples who are meant to be together let life pull them apart and blind them to their true feelings. That's what has happened with Emily and Lucas.

Lucas is hesitant to take his dream job because his ex-wife works at the hospital—but how can he turn down an offer to make real advances in brain injury research when that's his life's passion? Emily was his best friend once upon a time. Surely they can make peace and have an amicable work relationship? Only once he spends time with Emily he wants much more than just a work relationship with his ex. He wants *her*.

When her ex buys a date with her at a charity bachelorette auction Emily is reminded of all the things that made her fall in love with Lucas to begin with. Only this time around she isn't young, naïve, and blinded by visions of happily-ever-after. This time she won't let him anywhere near her heart. Only what if he's had it all along…?

I had so much fun on Emily and Lucas's journey to healing and happy-ever-after. I hope you enjoy their story as much as I did. I'd love to hear what you thought of their romance at Janice@janicelynn.net.

Happy reading,

*Janice Lynn*

# SIZZLING NIGHTS WITH WITH DR OFF-LIMITS

BY
JANICE LYNN

Published in Great Britain 2016
By Mills & Boon, an imprint of HarperCollins*Publishers*
1 London Bridge Street, London, SE1 9GF

© 2016 Janice Lynn

ISBN: 978-0-263-91511-2

**Janice Lynn** has a Masters in Nursing from Vanderbilt University, and works as a nurse practitioner in a family practice. She lives in the southern United States with her husband, their four children, their Jack Russell—appropriately named Trouble—and a lot of unnamed dust bunnies that have moved in since she started her writing career. To find out more about Janice and her writing visit janicelynn.com.

### Books by Janice Lynn

### Mills & Boon Medical Romance

*The Nurse Who Saved Christmas*
*The Doctor's Damsel in Distress*
*Flirting with the Society Doctor*
*Challenging the Nurse's Rules*
*NYC Angels: Heiress's Baby Scandal*
*The ER's Newest Dad*
*After the Christmas Party…*
*Flirting with the Doc of Her Dreams*
*New York Doc to Blushing Bride*
*Winter Wedding in Vegas*

Visit the Author Profile page at millsandboon.co.uk for more titles.

**Janice won The National Readers' Choice Award for her first book**
***The Doctor's Pregnancy Bombshell***

To Reesee. Love you to the moon and back!
Love, SMOM.

**Praise for
Janice Lynn**

# CHAPTER ONE

No. No. *No.* Her ex-husband *hadn't* just made an outlandish bid for Emily Stewart's Manhattan Memorial Children's Hospital Traumatic Brain Injury fund-raiser bachelorette date.

Lucas couldn't. Wouldn't.

Oohs and aahs were sounding around the hotel ballroom as the auctioneer expressed his excitement over the enormous leap in the bid. Emily just wanted to cry, *Noooooooo.*

She'd never dreamed of putting in a clause that said if her ex-husband lost his mind, bid and probably just won, her donated "date" was null and void. Then again, when she'd first volunteered with the fund-raiser, she'd not seen Lucas in five years. She couldn't possibly have expected him to show up at the auction, much less bid outrageously for her bachelorette number.

What she'd expected was her boyfriend to buy the date.

The reality was she'd been worried Richard would be her only bidder.

If only he had.

Why had she let Meghan convince her to do the auction? Standing on a stage letting men bid on a date with her was not her thing. Still, it had been for a great cause she believed in and she hadn't had the heart to say no despite fear of humiliation and embarrassment.

But if she'd known Lucas would show up and bid on her, no way would she have agreed to participate.

Ugh.

If she had one of those auction number thingies, she'd bid on herself. Could a girl do that?

White-knuckled, she forced a smile to stay on her face, but her cheeks were starting to hurt. Then again, that could be from her gritted teeth rather than her fake smile.

She dug her fingers into her palms and pretended everything was just fine, as if the man who'd once ripped her heart to shreds hadn't just bid a ridiculous sum to go to dinner with her.

He hadn't eaten with her when it hadn't cost him a thing except his time. Why would he want to now? After all these years? For that matter, why had he even taken the job at Children's? Manhattan was big enough for the both of them. Barely. Their paths should never, or at least rarely, cross. They'd been apart five years and, although she occasionally heard his name or saw a photo of him come across one of their few mutual acquaintances' social media page, she'd not seen him in person since the day their divorce had been finalized.

Until this past month.

Now she saw him every time she worked.

The auctioneer resumed his rapid-fire words, calling for another bid. Emily's gaze went to Richard, silently pleading with him to outbid Lucas. He might not have Lucas's millions, but the bid was far from being outside his reach. Why wasn't he stepping up, letting Lucas know she was his?

One of the auction volunteers walked over to stand near Richard, encouraging him to up the ante. But rather than do so, he shrugged and said something she could only make out bits and pieces of from where she stood on stage. What she caught was that the auction was "all for fun" and "for a good cause."

Cheeks on fire, forced smile glued in place, heart pounding out of her chest, Emily wanted to disappear. Richard made a good living. He could afford to bid higher. As her boyfriend, he should be bidding higher.

"Anyone else, folks? Come on, just look at her. Imagine a night out on the town with this gorgeous woman on your arm." The auctioneer turned his attention back to the rest of the crowd, trying to entice a new bidder into the ring. As if anyone else was going to cough up that much money to oust Lucas's high bid when her own boyfriend wouldn't. Ugh. This was humiliating.

"Going once," the auctioneer warned. "Going twice."

Her cheeks were so hot maybe she'd just spontaneously combust. Then sharing a meal with Lucas wouldn't even be an issue.

"Sold to the lucky gentleman holding number 146," the auctioneer crooned.

Great. Lucas had just won her date.

Emily walked across the stage to where the other auctioned-off women waited while the next bachelorette took center stage. In just a few minutes Emily would have to have a photo taken with her ex-husband. She'd have to stand next to him, smile at the camera and pretend she wasn't dying on the inside.

Thanks to his winning bid she had to sit through a meal with him across the table.

How dared he do this to her? Hadn't he caused enough havoc already to last a lifetime?

No.

Just no.

She was not having a meal with her ex-husband. Just the thought made her want to barf.

She'd play nice for the picture, but she would make a matching donation to the charity and wiggle out of the date. Although, Lucas had certainly been generous enough that doing so would make a painful dent in her savings. Still, the charity and avoiding time with her ex-husband were worthy causes.

*Why?* she wanted to scream at him from across the crowded luxury hotel ballroom. The hundreds of attendees might as well have not existed. All she saw was Lucas, smiling so nonchalantly, as if he hadn't just done something so absolutely wrong. Dressed in his tux, he was so handsome she wanted to shake her fist and yell it wasn't fair that he looked even better than he had when he'd been hers.

Their divorce hadn't left him any worse for wear. She'd been the devastated one who'd had to pick up the shattered bits of her heart and pretend her whole world hadn't fallen apart.

Her whole world had fallen apart.

But she'd survived, was stronger for the life lessons learned from her marriage to Dr. Lucas Cain.

Why had he drawn attention to himself, to her, by bidding such an out-of-the-ballpark amount for her date?

Why, when she'd finally put the pieces of her life back together, did he show up to throw rocks at her glass house?

She had made a good life at Children's, was dating and liked said boyfriend who'd not won her bid. Richard Givens, a pharmacist who worked near the hospital, was everything Lucas hadn't been.

She glanced Richard's way, saw him laughing at something someone at their table had said. Exasperation filled her. He'd just lost a date with his girlfriend to another man and he was laughing? Ugh. He wasn't worried. Why should he be? He didn't know Lucas was her ex-husband.

No one at Children's did.

Not wanting any reminder, she'd changed back to her maiden name and they'd never heard Lucas's name on her lips. Not until three weeks ago when he'd started in a medical director position at Children's pediatric neurology department. The department she worked in and loved. Maybe she could ask for a transfer.

Not having to see him would be worth giving up her beloved nursing position at Children's. Almost.

Anger flared.

How dared he show up where she worked and make her consider transferring positions when she'd already left one job to escape reminders of the biggest mistake she'd ever made? She'd left the hospital where they'd met during the end of his neurosurgery fellowship.

She should have known better than to marry Lucas.

She had known better.

Her parents had warned her. Her friends had warned her. His parents had warned her. His friends had warned her. No one had thought they should marry. She was too young, Lucas wasn't ready to settle down, they were too different and from too-different lifestyles. She'd been an ordinary middle-class girl from Brooklyn. Lucas had been born with a silver spoon in his mouth and had never had to stress over anything.

But she'd paid no heed. She'd been in love and thought she'd found her happily-ever-after at twenty-one.

She'd just graduated from her nursing program and had been at the hospital for only a few weeks when the most handsome man she'd ever seen had stolen her breath with his quick smile, mischievous eyes and quick wit. They'd had a whirlwind romance, then married and settled into her little apartment close to the hospital, because she'd refused to move into his parents' Park Avenue penthouse as he'd apparently thought they would. No, she had not wanted to start out her marriage living with her in-laws, whom she'd met only a couple of times. She'd planned to prove all the naysayers wrong over the next fifty-plus years.

She'd been the one proved wrong.

Wrong when Lucas had become less and less enamored

with their marriage no matter what she'd done to try to keep things smooth. She'd not expected a lot of his attention. He'd been in the midst of his fellowship, after all. But she had expected him to occasionally make time for his young wife, who'd loved him so much. Near the end, she'd barely seen him, had wondered if he'd even noticed she'd moved out of the apartment as he'd asked her to.

He must have. He'd immediately filed for divorce. For irreconcilable differences and abandonment.

Who'd abandoned whom?

She'd given him her heart, had put all she'd had into making her marriage a success, and he'd discarded her like yesterday's trash.

She'd sunk into a deeper and deeper depression, but nothing had ever hurt the way the demise of her marriage had, the way he had pierced her heart and bled it dry. Now that she'd carefully nurtured herself back into some semblance of a living, breathing person, had he come back to take shots at her a second time?

She wouldn't let him.

Her insides seethed with bitterness.

He couldn't steal her happiness or her peace of mind.

Only, from the moment she'd found out who had accepted the department position, her peace of mind had become a war zone. But it was a battle she would fight and win. She wouldn't give him so much power over her. Not ever again.

She'd planned to avoid him, to not interact any more than absolutely necessary to effectively perform her job duties.

Apparently, Lucas had other ideas. Like a date he'd very publicly paid too much money to beat Richard to secure.

While the current bid came to a close, Emily glared at her ex-husband, wondering if you could hate someone you used to love more than life itself.

He was no doubt considered quite the catch. She knew

better. She knew his flaws, knew that behind that handsome exterior beat the heart of a man incapable of loving another human being, of a man incapable of being there when his wife had needed him.

A man who hadn't been there on the worst night of her life.

Had he been at the hospital working, at his parents' or out partying with his buddies when her world had crumbled? Either way, he hadn't been at her side in that emergency room.

"Lucky you, girl!" Emily's best friend, Meghan, whispered. "I can't believe Dr. Cain just bought your basket. And for that price? You must be giving off some major pheromones or something because for a few minutes I thought he and Richard were going to come to blows."

Emily had never thought that. Lucas had never fought for her. He'd never fought for anything in his whole life. He wanted something and it just fell perfectly into place in his perfect life. She was probably the only mar on his stellar record.

And Richard, well, he was a nonconfrontational beta kind of guy, so she hadn't been too surprised when he'd let Lucas win the bid. Disappointed, but not really shocked. He would find paying such an exorbitant amount for something he did several times a week for free as a total waste.

Emily would have been highly impressed had Richard stepped up and rescued her from Lucas's bidding clutches. A knight in shining armor to her damsel in distress. Too bad. She'd have enjoyed Richard putting Lucas in his place.

To be fair, Lucas had raised the bid a stupid amount and Richard didn't have a deep trust fund to line his pockets, but the bid hadn't been out of his financial reach. Not by a long shot. Still, he worked hard for his money, was someone whom Emily could relate to. Richard was the same as her, an ordinary person living an ordinary life. She liked it that way.

"You can have him," she muttered under her breath to her fellow pediatric neuro nurse.

"Are you blind?" Meghan's expression was incredulous as they exited the stage to make room for the bachelors to be auctioned off. "He's the hottest thing to hit Manhattan since the term Big Apple was first coined."

Stepping a few feet away from the stage, Emily wrinkled her nose. Looks could be so deceiving. "He's not my type."

"Girl, he is every red-blooded female's type." Meghan waggled her perfectly drawn brows. "Tall, dark and handsome."

"To each her own, because he isn't mine. I prefer Richard."

This time it was Meghan's nose that wrinkled. "Richard is boring."

Emily frowned. "Richard is loyal, handsome, intelligent, kind—"

"You deserve so much better than the likes of Richard," her best friend assured her. Meghan had never understood her attraction to Richard, always claiming that she felt he stifled Emily.

"Not to me, he isn't." She'd had excitement and the fast lane while married to Lucas. She didn't need parties and a revolving-door social life. She liked going home to her apartment after her shift ended, cooking a light dinner for two, discussing their day and occasionally going for a walk or perhaps to a show.

Richard was calm, predictable, stable. Totally to her taste in men.

Totally and completely the opposite of Lucas.

"You can't tell me Richard is even in the same league as Lucas Cain."

"You're right, he's not. Richard is way above it."

Meghan gave her an odd look. "You been drinking?"

Emily laughed. "Because I find the man I'm dating more attractive than some new doctor at the hospital, you think I'm inebriated? Richard is my boyfriend. Why wouldn't I find him more attractive than Dr. Cain?"

"Do you?" a familiar male voice asked from behind her.

Every cell in Emily's body did a nervous jump to attention, making her legs weak, making her hands tremble, making her heart race. Not wanting to look at him, not wanting to have a conversation with him, she turned to face her ex-husband.

Up close he looked even better than he had from across the room. Why, oh, why couldn't time have taken its toll and marred the physical beauty of his face?

*He told you to leave. He filed for divorce. He's a cold, heartless jerk who means nothing to you.*

Even so, her hands shook and her stomach threatened to hurl the appetizers she'd consumed earlier. "Do I what?"

"Find the man who bid against me more attractive?" His blue eyes twinkled with the same old arrogant mischief. He knew that he was handsome as sin, that women fell to their knees when he so much as bestowed a smile upon them. He couldn't fathom her finding any man more attractive. The jerk.

"Of course I find Richard more attractive, Dr. Cain." She put great emphasis on her formal use of his name. "He and I have been dating for almost ten months."

"Ten months?" He raised a brow as if impressed as his gaze took in everything about her. "Some marriages don't last that long."

Her breath lodged in her throat and she dug her fingernails harder into her palms. Mentally, she called him every rotten name she could think of.

"You're right," she agreed. "Too many people get married who shouldn't. Probably because they're too young to know any better or one of them wasn't committed to the relationship to begin with. My guess is that when those people become involved in their next serious relationship, they are a lot choosier."

The arrogant look in his eyes flickered just a little, as if she'd delivered a damaging blow and won that round. Good. He needed taking down a peg or two.

"I bet you're right." He turned to Meghan and gave her a smile so charming that it was a wonder she didn't swoon. "Hi, I'm Dr. Lucas Cain. I work at Children's with Emily."

Ugh. He sounded so nice, so polite, and Meghan was tripping over herself trying to form coherent sentences. He'd always had that effect on women. Even her.

But that had been in the past. These days her sentences were freaking pieces of grammatical art. She'd been inoculated against his sexual mojo.

Well, mostly. He was a sexy beast and her body wasn't dead. Good thing her mind knew better and ruled.

"Me, too," Meghan practically stuttered. "At Children's. I mean, I work at Children's, too."

Lucas's brow lifted. "On the neuro floor with Emily?"

Hearing her name on his lips caused tightness to squeeze Emily's chest. Darn him that he was here creating chaos in her world, not to mention making a blabbering idiot of her best friend.

Meghan nodded, still stammering and stuttering. "I've taken care of a few of your patients."

He flashed one of his most potent smiles and Emily had to forgive her friend. When he was more handsome than anything Hollywood had ever put on the silver screen, how was Meghan supposed to resist? Her friend didn't know he had a heart of ice and a soul as black as coal.

"Ah," he said. "That's why you look familiar."

Emily wasn't buying that he hadn't known who Meghan was. No doubt he knew everything about her best friend.

Meghan's lashes swooped downward. "I guess you heard what I was saying about how you looked."

Her best friend was flirting with her ex. Not that Meghan knew, but still. Gag. Gag. Gag.

Just take Emily out and push her in front of a taxi driver right now. She couldn't take any more.

"If you'll excuse me, I need to go find a ladies' room." She went to move past Lucas, but the photographer chose that moment to appear.

"Hello," the overly friendly guy said, smiling and motioning for Lucas and Emily to pose. "Get together for a photo for our website."

Emily clenched her teeth and moved one step closer to Lucas.

The photographer frowned. "Smile. Look happy. You just brought in more money than any of the others."

There was that. Raising money for a good cause did make her happy. She sighed and focused on the help that would be provided to her patients' families because of Lucas's generosity.

Surprisingly, he looked a little hesitant. Lucas off guard. Now, that was something new. Still, he put his arm at her waist and smiled for the camera.

Trying to ignore the fact that he was touching her, Emily curved her lips upward.

The photographer's flash went off a couple of times.

"Thanks." The photographer turned to Meghan and her winner, who'd joined them. "Your turn, Pretty Lady."

Meghan curled up next to the stockbroker she'd gone on a couple of dates with.

Which moved everyone's attention off Emily and Lucas.

Her throat suddenly tight, she glared at him. "Congratulations. You're such a winner."

# CHAPTER TWO

THAT HADN'T GONE anywhere near the way Lucas had mentally rehearsed his first encounter with Emily outside the hospital.

Then again, what had he expected? He should thank his lucky stars that she hadn't made a scene.

The look she'd given him said she'd like to have smacked him. Or worse.

"I think you two got off on the wrong foot." Meghan rejoined him after the photographer had snapped a few shots of her and her date winner. The brunette frowned after Emily. "I don't understand how that's even possible. Emily gets along with everyone. She's the sweetest, kindest person I know."

They hadn't gotten off on the wrong foot, but they'd ended that way.

He closed his eyes and inhaled a deep breath, catching the faintest whiff of Emily's perfume still on the air. She'd always worn the light vanilla scent. He could never smell anything even close to the fragrance without being haunted by memories of the past.

Lately, most everything had his mind filling with Emily.

Ever since he'd been offered the position at Children's, he'd been confronted with memory after memory. Probably because he'd known taking the job meant coming face-to-face with his biggest regret.

To head the department, oversee research in traumatic brain injury, play an active role in the decisions being made that would impact how things were done on the pediatric neurology unit—Children's had offered him all that and more. The position was his dream come true.

He'd still hesitated.

Because of the woman walking away from him.

Just as she'd walked away five years ago.

Not that he hadn't deserved her leaving. He had. He just hadn't thought she'd walk away from their marriage, no matter how bad things got.

He'd been wrong.

But Emily had been right to leave. She'd been so unhappy, crying more often than not. Marriage to him had rapidly done that to her. He'd thought she was depressed, needing counseling, but when he'd suggested as much, she'd burst into tears. That night had been the night she'd packed her things.

His wife leaving him had hurt like hell, but he had gotten over it, had moved on and made a good life for himself.

But seeing Emily again had been tough. More so than he'd been prepared for. He wasn't sure quite what he'd expected of her, but the cold shoulder he got every time he walked onto the unit just had to go.

No, he didn't expect her to do cartwheels that he'd joined the hospital where she worked, but he was a good pediatric neurosurgeon and was now medical director of her unit. What had happened between them was a long time ago, water under the bridge, they'd both moved on. He was happy. She was happy. There was no need for awkwardness between them.

That was why he'd bid on her date.

Mostly.

As Emily's bid had proceeded, he'd grown more and more annoyed with the man she'd arrived with.

The man she'd been comparing him unfavorably to.

The man who'd acted as if bidding on Emily was an inconvenience.

Emily was too good for the guy.

He supposed it could be argued that she'd been too good for Lucas, too. She probably had been.

Besides, the guy must make her happy, since she'd defended him to her friend. Something Lucas had failed miserably at.

Regardless, the man's reticence to bid had irked. As he'd watched her on stage, the insecurities that only someone who knew her as well as he had would recognize flittering across her lovely face had brought out something protective.

So much so that he'd placed a bid. Then another, then, when her foolish date had hem-hawed on his last bid, Lucas had more than doubled the amount.

Probably not his brightest move.

But the guy needed to be hit over the head with the news that a date with Emily was worth every penny.

The realization hit Lucas hard.

He watched her retreating backside head out of the ballroom, appreciated the curvy lines of her body beneath the sleek lines of her formfitting emerald dress. Once upon a time, he'd slept with her backside snuggled into the curve of his body, spooned so close every breath he'd taken had been filled with her. Now he didn't have the right to even stroke his finger over the silky smooth skin of her cheek.

Lucas swallowed. Where had that thought come from?

He hadn't bid on Emily because he wanted a date with her. He didn't. He only wanted a chance to clear the air between them.

Maybe he'd been led to Children's so he could set the past right, could mend his relationship with Emily to where they could be friends, or at least amicable coworkers.

* * *

When Emily joined Richard at their table, his expression was sour and she cringed on the inside.

"Who was that man?"

She supposed she should have been prepared for his question, but it still caught her off guard. She'd run back to Richard to escape Lucas, not talk about him.

She bent, kissed her date's cheek. "No one, dear."

She wasn't lying. Lucas was no one. No one of any importance. Not anymore. Not ever again.

"He's interested in you." Richard didn't sound pleased. No wonder. Lucas had just upstaged him and their colleagues would be curious.

She sat in her chair and scooted closer to him. "He's new at the hospital and just drawing attention to himself."

Richard didn't look convinced. What he looked was annoyed. "By paying that crazy amount for you? Why would he do that?"

The money meant nothing to Lucas. He had paid too much. But did Richard really have to sound as if he found the idea that a date with her could possibly be worth so much as unfathomable? Shouldn't he find time with her priceless?

"It was for charity," she reminded him, irritated by his insensitivity to how she might take his question. "You said so yourself."

His expression pinched, Richard straightened the napkin in his lap. "I saw him talking to you a few minutes ago. Should I be worried?"

She laughed. "No. His type appalls me. Besides, all the bachelorettes took photos with the winning bidders. What did you want me to do? Refuse?"

Not that she wouldn't have liked to have done just that.

Richard's eyes narrowed beneath his wire-framed glasses. "You labeled his type in those few short minutes?"

"I've encountered him before." Ha. Wasn't that the understatement of the century? "He's a pediatric neurosurgeon in the department where I work. Actually, he's the new head of the department. He started about a month ago."

Twenty-two days.

Not that she was counting.

Emily shot a nervous glance toward where Lucas still stood with Meghan. They were both looking her way. Seeing her looking at them, Lucas lifted his glass in salute.

*The jerk.*

Emily rolled her eyes, grabbed Richard's hand and moved her chair to where her back was completely to Lucas. She didn't want him anywhere near her line of vision. She just wanted to forget he was even there.

Which later proved impossible even after Richard had quit talking about Lucas. He'd finally relaxed, quit suggesting she'd encouraged Lucas, and they were enjoying a slow dance. The emcee's boisterous voice cut in.

"Folks, it's time for our bachelors and bachelorettes to share a dance with their lucky high bidders." Applause went through the ballroom, but Emily didn't clap. Instead, she clung to Richard.

"Did you know they were going to do that?" He sounded aggravated, as if she'd somehow arranged the dance.

"No." She shook her head, wondering if she could make a mad dash toward the open double doors leading into the hallway. She could hide, freshen up in the ladies' room. "Maybe he won't come over here."

No such luck. Not that she had much hope of Lucas staying away. His new life mission was to irritate her as much as possible.

"Hello, Emily. I'm here to claim my dance." His gaze shifted to Richard's. "If that's okay with your date?"

She cringed. She did not want to dance with Lucas. Nor did she want to further upset Richard.

Hello. He'd been the one to let Lucas have the high bid. Couldn't he have spared more cash to have ensured she didn't spend time with any other man? Then again, Lucas might have just kept bidding higher and higher. Money meant nothing to him, except during the time when they'd been married and he'd been forced to live within their means rather than his parents'.

Maybe she was being overly sensitive of Richard. Maybe. Being around Lucas had her on edge, making her more critical than she should be.

She liked Richard. He was calm, soothing. He never rocked the boat, never made her question herself. Usually. Why was she letting Lucas disrupt her nice, content life? Letting him make her question a man she sincerely liked and had previously never fought with?

Her annoyance with her date was Lucas's fault, not Richard's. She needed to remember that.

Her gaze met Richard's. *Just say no*, she mentally pleaded. *Tell him to get lost. That I belong to you. That you refuse to share me. That I'm the love of your life and you'll never let another man take me into his arms.*

Richard didn't do any of those things. He just gave an exasperated sigh, stepped back and practically handed her to Lucas on a silver platter.

"Go ahead. All the others are," he said by way of justification.

So much for Richard going all macho and staking his claim. Not that she was the type to want the drama, but he could have at least issued some type of "she's mine, hands off" warning.

"He's a real winner, Em," Lucas teased as they stepped out onto the dance floor. "I see why you find him so attractive."

"Be quiet," she ordered, placing her arms around his neck. The feel of his body next to hers, the smell of him, the utter maleness of Lucas Cain, the memories of the past that hit her full force, almost had her forgetting about not making a scene and dashing out of the ballroom.

But she couldn't run away from him forever. She might as well find out what it was he wanted from her so he'd leave her alone. She didn't fool herself that he didn't want something.

Once upon a time, she had been what he wanted. That time hadn't lasted, had been more a tiny vapor that disappeared almost as quickly as it had appeared.

What was it these days that filled his dreams? That he wanted enough to come seek her out after all this time?

Had she accidentally taken a favorite shirt five years ago or something that he'd decided he just had to have back?

Too bad, so sad. Any clothes of his she'd accidentally taken had been donated to a local homeless shelter long ago.

Except for one shirt.

Memories assailed her.

Memories of going through a duffel bag she hadn't used in a long time and finding a T-shirt he'd bought at a concert they'd attended at Madison Square Garden. They'd been happy, dating, in love, laughing continuously, totally enamored with each other, believing nothing could ever come between them.

How wrong they'd been.

She'd shredded the T-shirt into pieces, hoping she'd feel better after doing so, but had only felt just as tattered as the bits of material.

"I'd have never let another man win your bid back when we were dating."

"No, probably not," she agreed, still fighting the urge to flee his arms. "But you'd have gift wrapped and hand delivered me after we were married."

Touching him was torture. Like being burned alive. Like

having a vise on her heart and it squeezing until every last drop bled forth.

"That's not true." His body stiff, his feet stopped moving for a few beats before resuming their dance. He looked torn, but then, rather than argue his point, he just sighed. "Let's not talk about the past anymore, Emily. Not right now. Let's just enjoy the song."

His capitulation surprised Emily. Before, he'd never have given in just to keep the peace. That had been her job. But he was right. They shouldn't talk about the past. The past was just that. The past. Done and gone forever. Best thing they could do was forget the past. It was what she'd been striving toward for five years.

She couldn't have said what song was playing prior to his calling her attention to it. A slow tune about second chances and new love. Ha. Emily never planned to fall in love again. Sure, she wanted someone to love her and to love, but she never planned to experience the craziness she'd had with Lucas.

That had been overwhelming, intense, too much for a heart to take when things fell apart.

She wasn't so naive as to think relationships lasted forever. Not anymore. Just look at most of the people she knew. Separated. Divorced. Achingly single.

Give her good old dependable Richard.

Sure, he didn't light any fires or even smell half as good as Lucas, but he wasn't a stick of dynamite burning at both ends, either.

"You smell nice, Emily."

Not something she expected to hear Lucas say. She misstepped and probably scuffed the black Italian leather dress shoes he wore. She didn't care. If she stomped his toes a dozen times, he deserved each and every smash.

"I don't know what you expect me to say." She didn't look up at him, just kept her eyes focused above his shoulders.

Her gaze collided with Richard's unhappy one.

Great. Trouble in paradise. Well, not paradise, but… trouble in Just Okay Land?

She inhaled sharply, then frowned at how her senses were overcome by Lucas. How could she have forgotten how good he smelled? Not that he wore cologne. At least, he hadn't in the past. Did he now? Maybe the light spicy scent was his aftershave? Or maybe his bodywash? Or maybe some expensive and pheromone-filled fragrance that guaranteed to drive women wild?

Not that he was driving her wild. He wasn't. Crazy did not equate to wild. Just…well, he smelled nice, too. And felt strong and solid next to her. Yes, her heart was beating wildly, but that really was just crazy.

"Honestly, I don't expect you to say anything. Nor did I mean to say it. The words just slipped out, but they are true. You do smell good. You always did." His breath brushed against her temple with soft, moist heat that prickled her skin with goose bumps. Why was he holding her so close? Why was she letting him?

She took a step back to put distance between their bodies. She hated that she reacted to him in any way.

If only every nerve cell in her body had quickly bored with Lucas.

"I didn't ask you for the walk down memory lane." The last thing she wanted was more memories. "You're the one who has instigated all this. You have no one to blame but yourself."

"That's true." His palm rested at the curve low on her back and pulled her close to him as they moved gently to the music. "I am the one who instigated our dance."

Emily's eyes narrowed. Had he bribed the emcee to announce the date-winner dance? Looking at him, she knew he had requested the dance.

"Why?" Did she even want to know? Probably not, but at least if she knew what he was up to, she could prepare a defense. She needed a defense.

"I could beat around the bush, but that's never been my style."

No, he'd always been blunt about whatever was on his mind. Like when he'd told her to move out of their apartment, for instance.

"This job at Children's is important to me."

His job. Of course this was about his job.

"I want everything to go as smoothly as possible, for nothing to stand in the way of my accomplishing the greatest good for our patients."

"You think I'd stand in the way of our patients getting good care because of you? How dare you imply that I'd ever not put my patients' needs before our petty past." She quit dancing. Probably because her feet felt heavy as concrete blocks. Her jaw dropped somewhere near the basement floor of the high-rise building. She stared up at him, wishing she could erase the past month, erase his having reentered her life. She'd been fine without him. She'd been good, healthy, content in her Just Okay Land relationship.

Lucas's gaze didn't waver from hers. "I don't think you'd intentionally do anything that would put our patients at risk."

"You think I might do something unintentionally?" she asked incredulously.

"No. What I think is that how you feel about me influences how you respond in front of our patients and coworkers. That could be problematic. That's why I bought your date, so we could talk and forge some type of friendship between us."

"You're crazy." He was crazy. Crazy to be at Children's.

Crazy to be at the fund-raiser. Crazy to have bid on her auction. Crazy to be on the dance floor with her in his arms. Divorced people didn't do this. She was sure of it. "You and I will never be friends."

"We at least need to forge some type of coexistence. There's too much tension and you run every time I come near."

"Perhaps you failed to get the memo, but I don't like you. Of course I leave when you're near."

"You think others haven't picked up on the tension between us?"

Why would anyone have paid attention to how she reacted to the new doctor? Before tonight. Now, after he'd bid such a stupid high amount, she suspected lots of people would be watching them to see if any sparks developed on their "date."

"I don't want you here," she snapped, wondering if anyone would notice if she stomped her high heel into his toes. His absurdity deserved a little pain. A lot of pain.

"I understand that," he clarified. "Knowing you were at Children's was my only hesitation. A mistake from five years ago shouldn't stand in the way of my dream job. I want to make peace with you."

She laughed. A louder than it should have been, close to hysteria laugh. "Let me get this straight. You bought my date because you want to make peace with me because of your dream job?"

His jaw worked back and forth. "Something like that."

Her hands went to her hips. "What if I already had my dream job and you pursuing your dream job is ruining mine? Why should I have to give up my dream job so you can pursue yours?"

"It's not as if I expect you to give up your job, Emily. Listen to what I am saying. I want us to coexist, maybe become friends." As if to prove his point, he pulled her back to him and began to sway to the music. She let him for the sole reason that standing in the middle of the dance floor with her hands on her hips squaring up to the man who'd just bought her date was just asking for people to stare. Anyone paying the slightest attention to her and Lucas was the last thing she wanted. Already, Richard couldn't take his eyes off them.

Obviously, Lucas didn't see a thing wrong with what he was saying. Or doing. That he was turning her world topsy-turvy. He thought it was okay to slow dance with his ex-wife and suggest they become friends. *The nerve.*

She closed her eyes, prayed she'd wake up and find the past month had just been a bad dream. "I cannot believe this."

"Why is it unbelievable that I want us to be friends?"

"We can never be friends," she hissed.

"Why not?"

"We were never friends to begin with."

"We were."

She shook her head. "You were never my friend."

"I'm sorry to hear that, because once upon a time you were my best friend."

His words gutted her and every cell in her body weighed down with lead, making movement almost impossible.

"Why couldn't you have just stayed in the past?"

"Because Children's offered me the position of medical director of the traumatic brain injury unit."

"I was here first." Even to her own ears her words sounded whiny and childish.

"I'm sorry that my being at Children's is problematic for you."

Two apologies in less than a minute. Wow.

"I'm not trying to force something on you, Emily. I just want the opportunity to make peace to where there isn't tension on the unit."

"I'm professional enough that I can hide my tension."

He sighed. "Then do it for me, please, because apparently I'm not."

"I owe you nothing," she stated.

"Then do it for our patients. I'm good at what I do. This position gives me the opportunity to do more. Let me."

As if she could stop him.

No hospital would give up a talented pediatric neurosurgeon just because a nurse, no matter how good she was, used to be married to him.

"Please."

Her gaze lifted to his and his sincerity surprised her. He didn't need her approval. They both knew it. So why did it matter? Why was he saying please? She didn't want to think he'd changed. She needed to keep him categorized in the "bad guy" box.

"None of this matters. What I think, what I want, doesn't matter," she reminded him. "You want this position, it's already yours. Just because I was here, loving my job and my life without you in it, doesn't matter to you. Nothing does except you getting what you want."

"This isn't just about me getting what I want. It's about doing the right thing, about what's best for all involved."

"Me coexisting with you is what's best for all involved?"

"You know it is."

She knew no such thing. Just being in his arms was driving her crazy, the feel of him, the smell of him, the sound of his voice. Okay, so her mind and body had gone a little mushy, but that was nostalgia, right? He'd been her first lover, her husband, her fantasy. Once upon a time, he'd been the center of her world and she'd have done anything to make him happy.

Her body had had a momentary lapse in memory, had responded to his spicy male scent, the feel of him against her, and, yes, she'd melted a little. A lot. But that was just old chemistry rising to the surface.

All she felt for him now was loathing.

*Liar.*

She squeezed her eyes shut and took another deep breath before meeting his gaze again with steely resolve. "This is ridiculous. You are ridiculous."

"Your heart is racing against mine, Emily."

He was right. Her heart was racing and was next to his, but what that had to do with anything, she wasn't sure. When had they moved so close that her body fully pressed against his as they swayed to the sultry beat? But she wasn't alone in being affected by the other one's presence. His heart was racing, too.

"Hearts race for a lot of reasons. Fear being one of them." Was that why his raced? She couldn't imagine Lucas ever being afraid of anything.

"Fear?" He looked taken aback. "I never gave you a reason to be afraid of me. Never."

He meant he'd never hit her or physically abused her in any way. He hadn't. The ways Lucas had hurt hadn't left visible scars, just jagged ones on the inside.

"Not any reason that could be physically seen." Emotionally, he'd beaten her to a pulp. She needed to remember that, to focus on how getting involved with him had devastated her whole world. She couldn't coexist with him. Not without severe consequences.

"You weren't the only one hurt by our marriage falling apart."

His words stung. He'd been hurt, too? Somehow she couldn't bring herself to believe him. He'd lost interest in her, in their marriage, long before the night he'd told her to leave.

How could he have hurt by losing something he'd no

longer wanted? By losing something he'd not even known about because he hadn't wanted to know?

Hadn't wanted, period. Had accused her of depression when in reality she'd been... No. She wasn't going there. She wasn't.

She glanced around the dance floor. No one was paying much attention to them. No one except Meghan, who gave her a thumbs-up when their gazes met.

*Oh, Meghan, if you only knew.*

She resumed scanning the crowd. Her gaze connected to Richard's again. She was going to have to do some explaining when she returned to the table.

Resentment built up in her and threatened to spill free.

"If you hurt, too, then why are you here opening up old wounds, Lucas? I've healed, am happy and could do without the twisted walk down memory lane."

She felt more than heard him swallow.

"I told you why I'm here."

"You and I will never be friends, Lucas. Leave me alone."

With that she stepped out of his arms and made her way back to where Richard waited. Richard, who clearly had a hundred questions waiting to spring from his mouth.

She didn't want to explain why she was upset about a shared dance with a man she worked with.

She bypassed the table and headed to the little girls' room.

Oh, yeah, she was happy.

# CHAPTER THREE

"HI, CASSIE. I'M DR. CAIN," Lucas introduced himself to the little girl he'd be doing surgery on soon if all went as expected. He'd spent a lot of time reviewing her medical records. She'd been diagnosed with a noncancerous brain tumor that had been increasing in size despite treatments to shrink the mass.

His true love within his field was traumatic brain injury, but he dealt with a lot of brain tumors and other brain maladies, too.

"Hi," the six-year-old answered, staring at him with big brown eyes that filled with uncertainty and a lack of trust.

No doubt over the past few months she'd been poked and prodded, tested and treated repeatedly to where she felt on constant guard long before his being asked to consult on her case by Dr. Edwards.

"What're you doing there?" He gestured to the puzzle she worked on.

She resumed scanning the puzzle pieces. "My mom says I need to do more puzzles. That it will keep my brain sharp."

"Your mom is a smart lady." He sat down at the table next to her. "Can I help?"

She shrugged. "If you want to. I'm not sure all the pieces are here. It's just a puzzle I found here, but it wasn't put together when I started."

Here being in the hospital playroom. A large room

equipped with kid-sized tables, video game stations, toy centers and table activity centers.

He sat at the table, seeming to search for a place to fit the puzzle piece he'd picked up. In reality, he studied Cassie, watching her movements, her facial expressions, how she moved her hands, her body. How she grimaced repeatedly when she tried to focus on what she was doing, how she squinted her eyes and had a slight tremor to her movements.

"Does your head hurt, Cassie?" The answer seemed obvious, but sometimes asking a child an obvious question, even one he already knew the answer to, could help break the ice. He wanted Cassie to trust him.

"Yes, but sometimes not too bad."

Her headaches were the first symptom that had clued her parents in to the fact that something wasn't right with their little girl. Never had they imagined they'd be told she had a brain tumor the size of a golf ball. Fortunately, Cassie's tumor wasn't cancerous, but, due to the size and the fact it was growing, she'd begun to have more and more problems. Visual changes, hearing changes, speech changes, motor-skill changes. She'd started falling for no reason other than poor balance. Because the mass was taking over vital brain tissue and causing increased pressure in her head.

Although it would be tricky due to where it was located within the brain and the amount of tissue it encompassed, Cassie needed surgical excision of the mass.

Lucas was the doctor who was going to perform the surgery.

"Are you going to take my blood?"

At the child's suspicious question, he shook his head. "No, I'm not here to take your blood, Cassie."

"I don't kick and scream," she told him, not looking up from her puzzle. "I used to, but I don't anymore."

"That's good to know, but I'm not going to take blood."

She cast him a dubious glance. "What are you going to do?"

"Right now? Help you put this puzzle together and talk about your headaches."

She shrugged. "Sometimes it feels like my head wants to blow up."

No doubt.

"I'm a pediatric neurosurgeon. My job is to make your head stop hurting."

The child looked up and squinted at him. "Can you do that?"

He nodded. "I've consulted with the neurologist you've been seeing, looked over your imaging tests. It's not going to be easy, but, yes, I believe I can make your headaches go away."

The child glanced toward her mother, who was sitting in a rocking chair watching their interaction. Looking tearful and tired, the woman nodded.

"I'd like my headaches to go away," the girl said.

"Me, too." He told the truth. Unfortunately, a lot of his cases weren't things he could correct or effectively treat. Once he removed the tumor, Cassie should get great relief.

Of course, nothing about brain surgery was ever that easy.

With removal of her tumor came a lot of risk. A lot of worry about what type of residual effects she'd have from his having removed a portion of her brain. Her tumor wasn't small and hadn't responded to the chemotherapy meant to shrink it. There was a chance Cassie would be permanently brain damaged after the surgery, that she wouldn't be able to do the things she currently did.

There was an even bigger chance that, at the rate her tumor was growing, the mass would take over her good tissue and cause more and more damage and eventually death.

Those were things he'd discussed with her parents in private already. They'd wanted to schedule surgery as soon as possible. He'd wanted to meet Cassie, to interact with her and to do a consult with a trusted pediatric neurosurgeon colleague to be sure he agreed with how Lucas intended to proceed with Cassie's care and predicted outcome.

He popped a puzzle piece into place. "Let's see if we can get this thing figured out."

She nodded and handed him another puzzle piece.

Emily stopped short when she entered the hospital playroom and saw Lucas sitting in one of the small chairs at a table where Cassie Bellows worked on a puzzle.

Emily took all her patients to heart. Cassie was no exception. Emily had instantly felt a connection to the little girl and her parents.

Especially Cassie's mother. Maybe because the woman was the same age as Emily. Maybe because of the gentle spirit she sensed within Cassie.

She'd known Lucas had been consulted on the case, knew that he'd likely do surgery on the child.

What she hadn't known or expected was to walk into the playroom and see a highly skilled pediatric neurosurgeon sitting at a child's table helping his patient put a puzzle together.

She'd worked in this department for years and that was one sight that had never before greeted her. If someone had told her she would see that, never would she have believed that neurosurgeon would be Lucas.

Lucas might have gone into pediatrics, but he'd given her the distinct impression during their marriage that he didn't like kids. Too bad he hadn't let her know that before…before… She sank her teeth into her lower lip.

He laughed at something the child said, then popped a puzzle piece into place, earning a "Good job" from Cassie.

The girl studied the connected pieces and quickly found another fit.

Lucas high-fived her, compensating when the little girl's movements were off from a sure smack of their hands.

Old dreams rattled inside Emily's chest and her eyes watered. A metallic tang warned she'd mutilated her lower lip.

Darn him. She didn't want to see him being nice. How was she supposed to keep him behind those "bad guy" walls she'd spent years erecting if he went around acting like a good guy?

It was an act. Had to be. He didn't even like or want kids. Not that he'd ever said he didn't like kids, but he'd reacted so poorly when she'd told him she wanted to have a baby. He had said point-blank he didn't want children and for her to stop talking about it. If only she could have. By that point, he had taken anything she said to him the wrong way, and she'd quit talking to him. Talking had led to crying and crying to arguing and arguing had led to more and more distance between them.

Currently, distance between them was what she desperately needed.

Having him at Children's was pure torture. Every time she saw him, she was taken to the past. She just wanted to forget the past. All of it.

Especially the end and the heart-wrenching events that had followed the night she'd left Lucas.

If only she could forget.

Why was he putting a puzzle together with Cassie? He didn't have to interact with the child. All he had to do was examine her, talk to her parents, get surgical releases signed and then do brain surgery. No. Big. Deal.

No interaction required.

He needed to stick with the program of how he was supposed to behave.

Instead, he played with the little girl while her mother

watched them as if he were a superhero. If Lucas cured
Cassie with minimal negative effects of removing the
tumor, she supposed Mrs. Bellows would find her views
justified.

Emily knew better. He wasn't a superhero, he was...

She stopped.

He was an ex-husband who was apparently a phenomenal pediatric neurosurgeon, and perhaps even a nice guy
to his patients if the vision before her could be believed.

Which she still didn't quite buy.

But Lucas was right about one thing.

If she was going to stay at Children's, she had to let go
of the personal. She couldn't let patients like Cassie and her
parents pick up on her animosity toward Lucas.

What if she caused them to doubt him? What if her feelings toward him somehow influenced a patient in a negative way and delayed or prevented needed care?

She'd told him she was a professional. She was. But even
professionals could have broken hearts blinding them from
time to time.

She couldn't allow her personal biases about Lucas to
bleed over to her patient care in any way. Not and remain
proud of the type of nurse she was.

She'd not seen him since Saturday night at the fund-
raiser. She'd managed to slip back into the ballroom and
convince Richard she'd developed a headache and would
like to go home. He'd looked relieved.

The headache had served as reason to send him home,
as well. That hadn't left him looking relieved. Quite the
opposite.

He'd acted as if he suddenly wanted to stake his claim.

Perhaps she should have let him stay.

She cared about him, had been thinking they'd have a
nice life together. He never made her cry.

But that night she hadn't even been able to tolerate the

idea of Richard kissing her. Nor had she been able to stomach the idea of him kissing her since.

She wasn't sure she'd ever want him to again, because just-okay-ever-after might not be good enough, after all.

Darn Lucas and the turmoil he'd caused. Saturday night and last night she'd dreamed about him, dreamed about the past. Not the tears or fights, but about the one part of their relationship that had been magical.

Sex.

She'd had no previous experience and sex had never been as mind-blowing since. How good things had been between them could only be credited to his skills. He'd made her feel amazing, loved, completely over the moon and satiated.

One touch of his hand had made her squirm with desire. One kiss from his lips had made her need him with a ferocity that had never failed to surprise her. One time with him and she'd been hooked like an addict with a potent new fix.

He'd been her drug.

Only, not long after their marriage, he'd bored of sex with her. Had he actually cheated on her?

She didn't think so.

Despite their flawed marriage, she didn't think he'd taken their vows that lightly. He'd told her to leave before he'd gone that far. Maybe she was being naive, but she truly didn't think he had.

In the days since their divorce, she didn't fool herself that he'd been abstinent. He'd enjoyed sex too much for that.

Darn him that just seeing him sitting and playing with a child had somehow morphed into thinking about sex. She wouldn't be having sex with Lucas. Not ever again.

Which was a shame in some ways, because he'd certainly made her feel things physically she'd not felt since. Richard really wasn't the guy for her. She needed to look for someone else, someone who wanted the same things out of life that she did, but was also good at sex.

Did such a mythical creature exist? So far her experience had been one or the other, but never the twain had met. She'd thought so with Lucas, but everything had fallen apart and left her devastated. So much for young love.

"You want to help with our puzzle?"

Emily blinked. Darn. He'd caught her staring at him and no wonder with how long she'd stood watching him, reminiscing about the past. Oh, yeah, Lucas being at Children's was affecting her professionalism, and she hated it.

"Sorry." Sorry she'd gotten caught. Sorry her cheeks were on fire. Sorry her mind had wandered. Sorry she couldn't be immune to him. Sorry her body flushed when he was looking at her as if he somehow knew what she'd been thinking. "I need to check on Cassie. She's due a vitals check."

The child looked at her suspiciously. "Are you going to take my blood?"

Focusing on her patient and doing her best to ignore the man watching her, Emily shook her head, hating that this was always the first question Cassie asked. Poor kid. "No. I'm going to take your temperature, your blood pressure, your heart rate, your oxygen saturation. Those kinds of things. But no needles."

Cassie digested her answer, then lifted her little chin bravely. "I don't cry anymore when my blood is drawn."

"That's a very big girl," Emily praised, wanting to wrap her arms around the child. "But it's okay to cry sometimes."

Cassie blinked. "Do you ever cry?"

She'd cried an ocean's worth of tears over the man sitting across the table from Cassie. Until Saturday night after she'd returned home from the TBI fund-raiser, she'd not cried in a long time.

She'd watered up on the anniversary of the day she'd left, but even then she'd managed to choke back the tears and keep herself distracted from the grief she knew she'd carry to the grave.

Unfortunately, a few days later, she'd broken down and cried bucketfuls. That had been the last day she'd cried. Maybe she'd always cry on that particular date. Oh, how much she'd lost.

"I used to cry a lot," she answered honestly. Lucas had hated her tears, had begged her not to cry, but usually that had left her only more tearful. "But I rarely cry these days."

Just when her ex-husband showed up and rocked her world by saying he wanted to be her friend. Right.

Lucas's gaze was intense, so much so it bore into her. She ignored him. Let him think what he wanted. She'd wondered if hormones had played into her constant tears, but perhaps Lucas had been the real cause.

"These days, what makes you cry, Emily?" Lucas asked, his fingers toying with the puzzle piece he held. Did he know she'd cried Saturday night? Did he want her to admit how much he'd affected her? Truly, he triggered strong emotions whether they were of happiness or sadness.

"Sad movies," she answered flippantly. No way was she getting into a discussion about what brought on her tears.

"Me, too," Cassie piped up and began to talk about a movie where a dog had died and she'd cried.

While Lucas watched, Emily removed the thermometer from the supply tray she carried. She took the girl's temp across her forehead, took her blood pressure, clipped the pulse oximeter over the child's finger and completed her vitals check.

Then she took her stethoscope and listened to the girl's heart and lung sounds and jotted them down on a notepad she kept in her pocket. She'd record them into the computer electronic medical record when she returned to the nurses' station.

"Is there anything you need, Cassie?" she asked.

Wincing a little, the little girl shook her head. "Just to finish this puzzle."

Emily glanced down at the three-fourths completed puzzle. "Looks like you're making good headway."

"Dr. Cain is helping."

"I'm not much help," Lucas quickly inserted. "Cassie is the puzzle master. I'm just riding on her coattails."

Emily's throat tightened. She didn't attempt to speak. Why bother? There was nothing to say even if he was kind to a child.

She fought to keep from frowning. *Professionalism*, she reminded herself. *Professionalism*.

Ugh. She had to get him out of her head.

Which had been a lot easier when he'd been out of her sight. Now that he was working at Children's, she was going to have to learn a new strategy to keep Lucas from ruining her hard-earned peace.

Work. She'd focus on work.

She turned to Cassie's mother, smiled. "Anything I can get for you, Mrs. Bellows?"

The woman shook her head and thanked Emily anyway.

Without a word to Lucas, she headed out of the room. Lucas joined her in the hallway seconds later.

"I'm sorry."

That made three apologies. Seemed Lucas's vocabulary had definitely expanded over the past five years.

"For?" she asked, not sure what it was that had him saying a word he used to be unable, or unwilling, to say.

"Saturday night."

Her heart raced within her chest, using her lungs for punching bags and leaving her breathy. "There were so many things you should be sorry for about Saturday night. Enlighten me as to which you refer specifically."

"All of it."

She ordered her hands not to shake and her feet not to trip over each other. "All of it?"

"Well, not the buying your date part," he amended, flashing a good imitation of a repentant smile. "I'd like to take you to dinner, Emily."

He wanted to take her to dinner. Flashbacks of the past hit again. He'd pursued her hot and heavy, had asked her out repeatedly until she'd said yes. Not that she'd not wanted to say yes to the handsome doctor, but she'd planned not to fall into the trap of dating the doctors she worked with. Ha. That hadn't turned out so well.

"Perhaps you misunderstood how the date works," she said, just because he waited for a response. "Part of what you won is that I am supposed to provide you with a meal."

"I'd rather provide you with a meal, but beggars can't be choosers. Would tomorrow night work?"

Beggars couldn't be choosers? What did he mean by that? Whether or not she agreed to coexist with him really didn't matter a hill of beans in his achieving his career goals. He had to know that. She frowned. "Maybe we should just make the 'date' a lunch one."

He shook his head. "I work through lunch most days and just grab a few bites of something when I can."

So did she, most days.

"Okay, fine. Tomorrow night," she agreed for the sole reason that the sooner she had her "date" with him, the sooner she had that behind her and wouldn't have it hanging over her head like an executioner's ax.

"Really?"

Why did he look so surprised? Then again, he didn't know she'd gone to the TBI fund-raiser chairman and requested to purchase her date and void her obligation to Lucas. The woman had denied her request with a laugh that said she thought Emily was silly for even asking.

"Let's get this over with."

His smile made his eyes twinkle. "What time can I pick you up?"

She did not want to be seen with him in public, but she supposed most of her friends already knew he'd bought her date. Several of them had asked how it felt to be bought by the hospital's hot new doctor. Ugh.

"I'll meet you at Stluka's." She told him the address of the bar and grill that was not too far from her apartment.

"Sounds great." He smiled and Emily's brain turned to mush. Pure mush. Lord, help her. She didn't want his smile affecting her, didn't want him to smile and her nerve endings to electrify with old memories.

That was all that was causing the zings through her. Old memories and not that he was knocking down bits and pieces of the protective wall she'd erected between them.

Maybe she was being too hard on herself. Lucas was a beautiful man with gorgeous eyes and a quick smile. Plus, she knew what those long fingers, that lush mouth, his hard body, were capable of. She knew.

Darn. She needed Lucas repellent. Or Lucas resistant spray. Or something. Anything to give her the power not to respond to his utter maleness.

She didn't want to respond to him.

He represented the worst time of her life.

He represented the best time of her life, a little voice reminded. Only, that time of joy had been short-lived and she'd spent years recovering from the aftermath.

# CHAPTER FOUR

EMILY ARRIVED AT Stluka's right on the dot of seven. Although she'd been ready and nervously pacing across her tiny apartment for the past hour, she'd refused to arrive early. She would not have Lucas thinking she'd been eager to spend time with him.

She wasn't.

She just wanted this over. Which didn't really explain why she had a nervous jittery feel in her stomach. Maybe that was normal when dining with one's ex-husband.

The perky blonde hostess greeted her with a huge smile and welcomed her to Stluka's. "Are you meeting someone or just want to hang at the bar?"

At that moment, a man stood from a bar stool, turned, met her gaze.

"I'm meeting someone. He's already here."

The girl followed Emily's gaze and gave an impressed look. "Lucky you."

Lucas joined her, but Emily wasn't sure if he overheard the girl's comment. If so, he didn't acknowledge her admiration.

"We're ready for our table," he told the hostess.

Smiling, she grabbed a couple of menus and motioned for them to follow.

The place was packed, just as it usually was, so the fact they were immediately being shown to a table surprised

Emily. Then again, there was no telling what Lucas had tipped the girl to have a table ready for them. Money talked.

"What are you thinking?" he asked as they walked toward a semiprivate booth.

"Nothing."

"Your expression went sour. Surely I haven't already done something to ruin your evening. I'd hoped you'd enjoy tonight."

"I'm not here to enjoy my evening, Lucas. I'm here to fulfill an obligation."

"And determined not to enjoy one moment of having to endure my company?"

"Something like that," she admitted, which garnered a low laugh from him.

He let her slide into the booth, then joined her. The hostess handed them the menus.

"Your waitress will be over in just a few minutes."

Lucas scanned the menu. "It all looks good. What's your favorite?"

She glanced briefly at her own menu. She did not want to make small talk, but the night would pass quicker if she at least attempted to interact.

"I like their cedar-plank salmon."

"Sounds good. That what you're getting?"

She nodded. "The apple-stuffed duck is really good, too."

"I'll order that, then, and share."

"I don't need you to share your food with me. I'll have my own."

"Maybe I was hoping to try the salmon and the duck so I'd know which I preferred for next time."

Next time. Would he be on a date? Have some young woman with him who wasn't so prickly, wasn't so five years ago.

"Suit yourself."

Their waitress came, took their order, then disappeared.

"Tell me, Emily, how did you end up in that bachelor/bachelorette auction? Even though it was for a great cause, I will admit, I was surprised to see your name."

She bristled. "Why? Think no one would bid on me?"

"I bid on you."

"It would have been better if you hadn't."

"Would you have agreed to dinner with me if not for the auction?"

"No."

"Then it was best that I bid. Besides, your guy was ticking me off that he barely upped the bid each time someone bid."

Yeah, there was that. Speaking of ticked off, Richard had not been happy that she'd canceled their plans that evening so that she could go out with Lucas. Actually, he'd been downright surly.

"That's why you jumped the bid out of his ballpark? Because he was barely upping the amount?" She'd just been happy that Richard had kept bidding against the strangers who'd been bidding prior to Lucas putting an end to all other interest.

"You deserve someone who sees your worth, Emily."

"Yes, I do, which doesn't explain why *you* bid on me." She immediately wished she could retract her words. She didn't want to argue with Lucas. She wanted to make it through dinner and go home unscathed from spending time in his company.

"Ouch."

"The truth often hurts."

"True." He took a sip from the glass of water the waitress had set on the table. "If I was completely honest, I'd admit that I didn't know I was going to bid, until I actually did."

He hadn't meant to bid on her? She wasn't sure if that made her feel better or worse that he had.

"Like I said, you shouldn't have." She unfolded her

napkin and put the cloth in her lap. "All it's done is cause problems."

"How so?"

"Richard is my boyfriend. He isn't thrilled at what you did. Nor is he thrilled that I'm out with you tonight."

"He could have bid higher." He took another drink of water.

"He could have," she admitted, wondering why she was defending Richard. He could easily have afforded to bid higher and he should have. That he hadn't irked her. Never would she have let another woman win a "date" with her man when she had the means to prevent it. "But Richard is way too practical to spend that much money on dinner with me. Why should he when he knows he gets to spend time with me for free?"

"You like practical?"

"I love practical," she immediately answered. She did like practical. Impractical made her feel out of control and that was something she never wanted to be again.

Lucas coughed as if his water had lingered and gone down the wrong pipe. "You love that guy?"

She wanted to lie. She wanted to say she was madly in love with Richard. She wanted to be able to tell Lucas that, yes, she had moved on past him and given her heart to another.

Instead, she told the truth.

"Richard is a great guy." Despite how surly he was over Lucas. Then again, Lucas was a handsome doctor; under different circumstances that didn't involve a past relationship that had ended in divorce, Richard would have every right to be surly. Maybe she should tell him who Lucas really was. "We have a lot in common and I enjoy our relationship."

At least, she had right up until Richard had let Lucas

walk away with the winning bid without even putting up a fight. Now she found herself questioning everything.

Lucas's gaze didn't waver from hers. "But do you love him?"

Did she love him? Not in the way Lucas meant. Not in the way she'd loved him. She'd never let herself love that way again. She knew how much that kind of love hurt.

"I don't think my feelings toward Richard are any of your business."

"You don't." He leaned back against the booth seat and studied her. "You're not in love with him."

At first she thought he sounded smug with his claim, then she realized he was saying the words as much for himself as he was to her. Which had her wondering why. Why would Lucas care if she was in love with Richard? He hadn't come to Children's because of any lingering feelings for her. He'd come because he'd been given a medical director position that was his dream job.

"What do your parents think of him?"

"They like him." Mostly. Part of her knew her parents were just glad she was out and dating, that she was rebuilding a life for herself. Plus, Richard was a pharmacist, a good man with a steady income, and he came from a similar background to Emily. They liked that about him. They liked that he wasn't Lucas. They'd die if they knew she was out with him, that he'd come to work at Children's. Her mother would be trying to get her to change jobs immediately. Her father would, dear Lord, her father would likely come after Lucas if he knew she was within ten feet of the man who'd broken his little girl's heart.

"How about you?" she asked, wanting the conversation to turn away from her and Richard, to turn away from her parents and how they, probably rightly so, felt about Lucas. "Anyone special in your life?"

He shrugged. "I date from time to time but am currently not seeing anyone."

"Maybe you'll meet someone at Children's and sweep her off her feet and live happily ever after."

Why did the thought of him meeting someone and her having to watch that relationship blossom make her physically ill?

"I'm not looking to meet anyone, Emily. I'm at Children's because of the career and research opportunities being there provide me. Nothing more."

Nothing more. As in, she shouldn't get any ideas he was there because of her. Ha. As if. She knew better than that. He'd expressed himself loud and clear on that one over five years ago. "What type of research opportunities?"

His eyes lighting, he told her about a new procedure he and a colleague had been developing to reduce intracranial pressure post head trauma. His passion for what he was doing, what he hoped to achieve, impressed Emily. Lucas loved what he did and wanted to make a difference in his patients' lives. Darn him. She didn't want to like anything about him, but she admired his passion.

"You couldn't do that at where you were before?"

He shook his head. "Dr. Collins is still the medical director and shot me down every time I wanted to use the procedure."

Dr. Collins. A grumpy old man who was so antiquated he must have come with the building. No wonder a progressive neurosurgeon like Lucas had sought other career opportunities.

"At Children's you get to make the final call of whether or not the procedure takes place?"

"I'm just waiting for the right patient."

"What's the advantage over traditional procedures to decrease ICP?"

"It's less invasive and less risk of post-surgical complications." He explained the procedure and continued to do so after their meal arrived, pausing only to brag about how good the duck was.

Surprisingly, Emily found herself enjoying listening to Lucas.

"I didn't know you were so interested in research."

He shrugged. "It's always been a dream."

"I never knew that."

"We didn't talk about my school and work much."

"We didn't talk much about anything," she reminded, more sarcasm than she'd meant coming out in her tone.

"That's not how I remember things. At least, it wasn't that way in the beginning. We'd spend hours just talking."

La. La. La. La. She fought to keep memories from rushing into her head. Memories of lying in Lucas's arms, naked, sated, and talking about anything and everything. Much easier to keep him at a distance if she only remembered the endless tears and screaming matches they'd battled through.

Seeming to realize that she was throwing up walls, he forked a piece of his duck, then held out the loaded utensil. "Here. Taste."

She shook her head. "I know it's good."

"Humor me so I won't feel guilty when I ask to try your salmon."

She did not want him to feed her, nor did she want to feed him. "But I…"

"Emily, please."

*Please.* The word on his lips undid a knot holding her emotions back. She leaned forward and took the bite he offered.

The sweet yet tart flavor of the apples next to the tender duck had Emily sighing. The salmon was her favorite, but the duck dish ran a close second.

"That's good."

His gaze dropped to her plate.

"Oh, all right." She forked a piece of the flaky pink meat and proffered her fork.

His gaze locked with hers, his mouth closed around her utensil, then he smiled. A real smile that reached his eyes and was full of pleasure.

Emily fought to keep her eyes open, hating the weakness surging through her. She didn't want to respond. Not in any way, shape or form.

But sharing his food, sharing her food, had her gulping.

"Amazing," he agreed, and she assumed he meant the food and not the starburst of feelings shooting through her. Why, oh, why couldn't she be immune to this man? She should be immune. He'd hurt her so badly, he shouldn't have any control over her feelings anymore. Not any.

"This was a really bad idea." She hadn't meant to make the admission out loud.

"Why?"

"You're my enemy."

"Your enemy?" He shook his head. "That's not who I am, nor how I see you, Emily."

"How do you see me, Lucas?"

Lucas studied the one woman he'd given his name to and who had held more power over him than any other. His wife. Ex-wife, he corrected.

"I see you as the most beautiful woman on the inside and out that I've ever met."

She was. If only her sadness hadn't taken over their relationship. If only he'd been able to understand and help her through whatever had changed within her. Him. He'd been what had changed her. No wonder she'd jumped at the chance to leave.

Emily's eyes closed and she shook her head. "Don't say things like that."

"Things like what?"

"Things you shouldn't say to me."

"Why shouldn't I tell you how beautiful you are?"

"Because you quit making me feel beautiful long ago."

Her words stunned him, shocked him, but maybe they shouldn't have. He and Emily had fallen apart. He regretted that he'd played any role in her not seeing the beauty so evident in everything about her. "I am sorry, Emily."

"I don't want your pity. It was a long time ago."

"I don't pity you. I pity myself at what I lost." His admission shocked him almost as much as hers had. He did regret that he hadn't been able to make Emily happy. When he looked across the table at her, saw the depth of emotion in her eyes, heard the sincerity in her voice when she spoke, he was filled with longings for her laughter, for her to smile at him the way she used to, before they'd married.

"Can I interest you in dessert?" the waitress asked, filling up Lucas's water glass.

Emily shook her head. "I'm full, but thank you."

Lucas found himself wanting to order dessert just so he could prolong the meal, could prolong his time with Emily, but he declined, also.

"Thank you for dinner. Everything was delicious," she told him so formally he cringed.

"You sound as if you're done."

"I am."

"The night doesn't have to end, Emily." At her look of horror, he elaborated. "I didn't mean we should have sex."

Although, he didn't find the idea nearly as horrific as she obviously did.

Because he still wanted her.

The realization was an earth-shattering one.

He still wanted Emily.

"Whatever you meant, my answer is no."

"You aren't curious about what I had in mind?"

She shook her head. "I just want this obligation over."

Which put him in his place.

The waitress set their check on the table, and when Emily went to grab it, he beat her to the ticket.

"You're not paying for our meal."

"But the fund-raiser…"

"Doesn't matter. You're not paying."

"But…"

"Emily, please don't argue on this one. Just let me feel like a man by paying for my date's dinner."

"But I'm not really your date."

"Sure you are. That's what I won. A date with a beautiful bachelorette to raise money for a great cause."

She glanced down at where her hands rested in her lap, then shrugged. "Okay, if that's what you want."

What he wanted was Emily.

She was his ex-wife, not a woman he was trying to woo or get to know better. He already knew Emily better than any woman in his life. Only, he didn't know her at all. Not anymore.

But he wanted to know her. Everything about her.

He finished his fresh glass of water, then nodded. "Yes, that's what I want."

When they'd split, he'd not been thinking clearly. He'd been spoiled, a kid still in many ways, focused on becoming a doctor, and when he'd had free time, he'd wanted to unwind, to hang with his fellow residents, his lifelong friends, to enjoy life and being young, not sitting inside the tiny apartment they'd called home and staring at the four walls. Or fighting, which was all they'd seemed able to do once they'd said I do.

What he should have been enjoying was Emily, but how could he do that when she'd cried almost nonstop, when he'd looked into her eyes and seen such horrific sadness that he hadn't been able to stand it?

She'd once been so bubbly. Within minutes of meeting her during his residency program, he'd become enamored with the perky nurse who knew her stuff and had the most enchanting smile and big green eyes he'd ever encountered. He'd been intrigued, asked her to go for coffee, and, although he could tell she was similarly intrigued, she'd refused.

He'd asked again the next day. And the next. And the day after that, too, even when he hadn't been working.

That day she'd said yes for the following day, if he was available. Although he'd had to do some major shuffling, he'd made himself available.

Over coffee they'd talked, laughed, ended up going for a walk in Central Park, and coffee had turned into dinner. She'd told him she'd said no not because she wasn't attracted to him, but because she'd just started at the hospital a few months before and really wasn't interested in becoming involved with someone who also worked at the hospital. When it had come time to tell her good-night, their kiss had been intense. He hadn't wanted to go, but she wouldn't let him stay.

Over the next few weeks, he'd spent every spare moment with her and quite a few he hadn't had to spare. The demands of his residency program, his family obligations and wanting to be with Emily nonstop started taking their toll. He pretty much gave up sleep, felt exhausted more often than not and knew he couldn't keep burning his candle at both ends. He'd thought if they married, it would ease the strain on several counts.

He'd been wrong.

She'd been trying to be the wife she'd thought she should be, but she hadn't connected with his family or his lifestyle, had insisted she live within her means instead. With each day that had passed, her smiles had become less and less frequent until they'd completely been replaced by tears.

He'd kept telling himself it would get better once he finished his residency, that he just had to bide his time.

Then she'd started talking about wanting a baby.

They'd been married less than a year. She would burst into tears within minutes of seeing him. He was in a medical school residency program. All they'd done was fight and have makeup sex. He'd talked with his parents and they'd accused Emily of being a gold digger, of trying to tie herself to his inheritance forever by having a baby. He hadn't believed them, not really. If Emily had been after money, why would she have insisted they live in her tiny apartment? To live within her income rather than the lavish lifestyle his trust could have provided? If his money was what she'd wanted, why was she so sad all the time? Because he'd have given her anything. He'd tried, had wanted to, but no matter what he'd done, it had been wrong. Being married to him had clinically depressed Emily. Not that she would admit it or agree to get help. How was that supposed to make a man feel? That being his wife made her ill?

He'd found himself backing away from their relationship. He'd barely been able to find time for the things he'd had to do, she'd cried all the time, and she'd been thinking about throwing an innocent baby into the mix?

If he'd been with Emily, he'd wanted her and had feared that she might end up pregnant on purpose. He'd started spending more time at the hospital, doing research, spending time with his parents, especially his mother, who'd been reeling from losing her mother a few months into his marriage to Emily, spending time with his friends, anything and anywhere to where he and Emily hadn't been alone, to where they couldn't have been intimate.

At first she'd gone with him to the things she could, had tried to keep up with his crazy, fast-paced schedule. Eventually, she'd quit, opting to go home. And do what? He really didn't know. Just that the emotional rift between them had kept dividing until it had reached mammoth proportions over just a few months.

And yet, for all the past, he wanted her even now. Just without the golden rings to choke out everything good between them, without that stress they'd put upon their once fantastic relationship, without the tears and the fights. He wanted what they'd had those first few months they'd been together and she'd been his best friend, his confidant, the person who had brightened his life in so many ways.

So long as they didn't put the expectations upon each other their wedding vows had burdened them with, they should be just fine.

In his mind, it all made perfect, logical sense, but when his gaze met Emily's across the table, he knew his logic and her logic weren't anywhere near on the same page.

# CHAPTER FIVE

EMILY WANTED TO SCREAM. Why did Lucas keep staring at her that way?

A way that had her questioning his motives.

A way that made her think he wanted to have her for dessert.

As if.

He paid for their food by tossing down a couple of large bills that no doubt made their waitress's night.

"No change? Really?" The young woman smiled hugely. "Thank you."

"Thank you for dinner, too," Emily added, standing. "I need to be going. I have to work tomorrow."

She needed to get away from Lucas. Seeing his kindness, his generosity, to the waitress bothered her. Not that she didn't want him to be generous. He could certainly afford to and generosity was a good thing. She just didn't want to witness any more "good guy" behavior. Nor did she want to make any more comparisons between Richard and Lucas. Richard was a "to the exact recommended percentage only" tipper and would have been appalled at what Lucas had given to the young woman. Just as he was appalled at how much Lucas had bid for tonight's "date."

"I'll walk you home."

"No."

"Emily," he began, but she shook her head.

"Lucas, you aren't going home with me."

"Walking you home and going home with you aren't the same thing."

"Either way, I walked myself here and I can walk myself back."

"You offend my gentlemanliness."

"Too bad, but you aren't getting anywhere near my apartment."

"Is being around me that bad?"

Why had his voice sounded off when he'd asked his question?

"Being around you isn't good."

"I'd like to prove that you're wrong about that," he said as they stepped outside Stluka's and onto the sidewalk. Although the street wasn't that crowded, at the end of the block they could see the hustle and bustle of Broad Street. "I think our being around each other could be good for both of us."

She paused walking. A man behind her excused himself and went around her as she glared at Lucas. "Why would you possibly think that?"

"We had a lot of passion and strong emotions between us that we were too young to deal with and we let our relationship fall apart. Life has thrown us back together for a reason."

"You're crazy."

"Yeah, maybe I am, because right now all I can think about is how much I've missed spending time with you. I suppose there are a lot of people who'd say that's pretty crazy."

"For the record, I'm one of those people. The only reason I'm spending time with you is because you won the auction. Don't mistake my being here as anything more."

"I don't believe you, Emily. I feel the vibe between us."

She glanced down the street, considered making a run for her apartment. How dared he call her bluff?

"You're still as attracted to me as I am to you."

"I'm not attracted to you at all. Whatever vibes you think you're picking up on all have to do with the past, Lucas. There's nothing between us in the present. Nothing at all. Good night."

Head held high, she walked away, praying her feet didn't trip up and make her land on her face because she felt his gaze on her retreat.

Some of Emily's patients truly broke her heart. Jenny Garcia was one. The four-year-old girl had been rushed to the emergency room after she'd been abused by her mother's drugged-out boyfriend. The child had sustained multiple injuries including broken ribs, a busted lip, blackened eyes and bruises all over her tiny body. She'd also suffered from a concussion and brain injury that had the emergency physician opting to admit the child onto the unit where Emily worked.

Lucas was the physician assigned to her case and he'd shown up on the floor just minutes after Emily got the unconscious girl checked onto the unit.

"How bad is she?"

"She's pitiful," Emily admitted, her eyes watering. No, she was not going to cry. She wasn't. She would not lapse into crying in front of Lucas. She was beyond that life phase.

"Some people shouldn't have children."

*Some people didn't.*

Emily flinched. Nope. Not going there. La. La. La. Not allowing those thoughts to enter her head.

"I agree." She handed him the computer tablet with the girl's information pulled up.

His wince tugged way deep inside Emily. Lucas sighed, then raked his fingers through his thick hair. "Where's the mom?"

Emily shrugged. "I've not seen her. One of the ER nurses said she was there for a while, but that she didn't stay."

"How could anyone leave their child after something like this happening?" Lucas asked, truly looking shocked.

Emily had had the same thought when the ER nurse had told her the girl's mother had left. Emily tried not to judge, but sometimes it was darn hard not to.

Lucas nodded. "Go with me to check her?"

Emily didn't want to go anywhere with Lucas, but she couldn't refuse the unit's medical director.

When his eyes touched on the child in the hospital bed, his disgust emanated.

"There are several consults already in the system besides yours," Emily told him. "The ER physician just felt having you look over her brain scans and getting her ICP down was the most imperative once they had her otherwise stabilized."

"She's going to need surgical repair of some of her injuries."

Emily nodded. "Jeremiah Franklin reset a bone and closed a few wounds prior to her transfer to the floor. He plans to take her back to surgery once you feel it's safe for him to do so."

"Noted." Lucas did a neuro check on the child from head to toe so he could assess the extent of her injuries. Emily had already completed a similar examination but watched Lucas's highly efficient but gentle exam. The child was unconscious and yet, still, his touch was nurturing and caring.

The girl moaned in pain, the sound barely above a tortured whimper.

"I'll kill the guy myself if he ever shows his face here."

Emily nodded. She felt the same. The absolute protectiveness Lucas was showing over the child stunned her, though.

He'd have made a great father.

A tortured whimper escaped her own lips at her thought and she turned away.

"I'm sorry, Emily. I shouldn't have said that out loud."

Forcing herself to face him, she shook her head. "No, for once, we agree on something. I'd like to introduce him to my dad's baseball bat."

A small smile toyed on Lucas's face. "I've heard about your dad's baseball bat."

Emily's gaze flickered to the child. "Yeah, well, too bad she doesn't have a dad with a baseball bat to have protected her from the world's bad guys."

"Agreed." He touched her shoulder, then let his hand fall away as if realizing he shouldn't be touching her. "I'm off to get prepped for surgery to release the pressure in her head. Pray all goes well and I have her back to you before your shift ends."

With more wires and bandages than she'd left with, Jenny returned to the unit about an hour before time for Emily's shift to end. She got the child settled, with all vitals checked and recorded.

Lucas looked over the information in the computer, then went to the girl's room and found Emily standing next to the child's bed and holding her hand.

His heart squeezed at the image, at the compassion on Emily's face. The look that said had this been her child she'd have protected her until her dying breath.

Once upon a time, Emily had wanted a child. His child. Did she plan to have children someday still?

As much as she'd talked about having a baby and starting a family, he was surprised she hadn't already.

Any child would be blessed to have her as a mother.

If only they were meeting now for the first time, without the past between them, how different would things be? Would he be looking at her right now and admiring her beauty, her compassion, her heart, and wondering at the emotions she elicited within him?

Would he ask her to dinner and commiserate over life's injustices that a child would suffer such a cruel fate? Would they bond and hold hands, hug each other, share their first kiss? Would they—

"Oh, sorry, I didn't see you there." Emily interrupted his thoughts, pulling her hand free from the child's and moving away from the hospital bed. "She's resting peacefully at the moment and her ICP pressure has improved a lot from prior to surgery. You used your new procedure on her. It seems to be working."

"So far, at any rate. She has a long way to go to recovery."

Emily nodded. "If you'll excuse me, I'm going to go check my other patient."

Lucas watched her walk across the room. Just as she made it to the door, he stopped her. "Go to dinner with me, Emily."

He hadn't known he was going to ask her, but more than anything he wanted her to say yes.

"I can't," she told him. "I already have plans."

"With the pharmacist?"

Not meeting his gaze, she nodded.

"Will you understand if I don't say to have a good time?"

Her gaze lifted to his. "Not really."

He sighed. "Go, Emily. Have a good time. The best."

Emily didn't have the best time. Richard was quiet, sulky, wanting her to pay penance for having dinner with Lucas the night before. She kept having to remind herself that Richard wasn't the problem. Lucas was.

She smiled across the dinner table, forced herself to listen to him recount a story one of his pharmacy customers had told him that day. She hadn't had to force herself to listen to Lucas the night before. She'd soaked up every excited word he'd said. He'd talked with such passion about his career, about the new procedure and the research he planned to do at Children's.

"Emily?" Richard cleared his throat loudly. "I asked what you thought about that."

"Sorry." She was even more sorry because she had no clue what he was referring to. No matter as he launched back into another recount of the tale. Emily tried to remain attentive to what he was saying, but instead her thoughts drifted back to Lucas.

Where was he? Still at the hospital or had he perhaps made plans with someone else?

Why had he asked her to go eat? They'd worked together amicably enough that day. She hadn't run off when he'd shown up on the unit, which was what she gathered his purpose in buying her bachelorette date had been. What would be the point in going to eat a second time?

Her phone buzzed in her purse that sat in the chair beside her. While keeping her gaze trained on Richard, she slid the purse into her lap and removed the phone. With a quick swipe of her finger she opened the screen, glanced down and hit the message button. She didn't recognize the number, but she knew who the message was from.

You look bored.

How do you know? she typed back.

Just hungry and ended up at the same place as you.

Hard to believe that's coincidental.

Yet it is.

"Emily, am I boring you?"

She glanced up at the man across the table from her. "Sorry, I had a message I needed to answer."

"Work?"

Heat flooded her face. "Yes, someone from work."

Oops. Sorry. Someone looks upset. Guess I better quit bothering you.

Yes, you should.

You should have said yes when I asked you to dinner.

Why?

Because you'd be having a better time.

With you? I don't think so.

We should test that theory. Don't make plans with him tomorrow night.

Leave me alone, Lucas.

Please.

Ugh. There was that word again. When had he learned to use it so proficiently?

"Everything okay?" Richard asked, causing her to glance up from her phone.

"Yeah, just had a long day today."

"Anything you want to talk about?"

"No," she admitted, realizing she didn't want to tell Richard about her day.

"Were you out that late last night? No one forced you to

participate in the fund-raiser," he reminded her, his voice full of condemnation. Again.

"No, I wasn't out that late last night, and no one forced you to let someone else win my bid."

Ouch. Had she really just said that out loud? She hadn't meant to. She'd meant to keep her feelings quietly under wraps. Even if Lucas had pointed it out. Even if Lucas was probably watching her argue with Richard.

Richard's lips compressed into a tight line. "If you'd wanted me to buy your bid, you should have told me."

Practical. Logical. Infuriating.

"Really? I shouldn't have to tell you that I wanted you, the man I'm dating, to win my bid."

His voice had taken on a truly confused tone. "Then how was I supposed to know?"

"You shouldn't want me going to dinner with another man."

"I don't want you going to dinner with another man, but you went anyway."

"Then you should have bought my date so I wouldn't have had to." She pushed her plate away. "I'm tired and ready to go home."

He frowned but put his napkin down. "We can leave as soon as I pay the bill."

"Good. Great. The sooner the better."

Why, oh, why did it bother her so much that he tipped their waitress to the exact penny of the recommended amount?

She'd barely had a couple of conversations with Lucas and he'd already managed to make her question her relationship with a man she'd been quite content with.

Content?

Since when was life about just being content?

When did she stop wanting happily-ever-after and the full-blown fairy tale?

She knew. She'd stopped believing, stopped dreaming, when her marriage to Lucas had fallen apart.

She fought to keep from looking around the restaurant to spot Lucas. Where he was didn't matter.

She and Richard walked back to her apartment in silence. She turned to him. "I'll just say good night down here."

"You're not letting me come up?"

She shook her head. "It really has been a long day."

"This isn't working for me, Emily."

She blinked at him. "What do you mean?"

"I mean, you going on dates with other men and then sending me home. I'm supposed to be the man in your life."

He was right. He was supposed to be the man in her life. Only, she wasn't sure she wanted him to be. Surely she deserved better than just the status quo.

"I think you need to reconsider or we need to consider taking a time-out from our relationship."

What? "If I don't invite you upstairs, we're through?"

He didn't answer, just stared at her with an expectant look on his face that was answer enough.

Well, at least he was making this decision easy.

"You're right. We do need a time-out from our relationship."

Surprise flittered across his face. He'd thought his ultimatum would result in an invitation into her bed?

"If you've set your sights on that doctor, Emily, you're wasting your time. You're throwing away a good thing for a man who's never going to take someone like you seriously."

"Someone like me?" He made it sound as if she weren't good enough for Lucas, as if she were lucky Richard found her appealing.

He shrugged. "You're not in his league."

Ouch.

Emily's lips curled into a forced smile. "Thanks for an

enlightening evening and for making what could have been a difficult moment into an easy one. Goodbye, Richard."

Emily was assigned to Cassie and to Jenny the following day. Cassie had continued to decline, but Jenny was holding her own. It would probably be a couple of days before the four-year-old regained consciousness, which was probably a good thing. Perhaps some of her injuries would have subsided a little.

"Her vitals remained good during the night."

She turned to the man entering the room. The man she'd lain in bed and thought about way too much the night before. Shouldn't she have been thinking about the man she'd just ended things with instead?

"Yes, she's stable."

"That's good news." He examined the unconscious little girl, then turned to Emily. "Give me more good news."

"Pardon?"

"Tell me you didn't make plans for tonight."

Emily sighed. "I'm not going to go to dinner with you, Lucas. There's no point."

"Is there a point to you going to dinner with the pharmacist?"

"Richard has nothing to do with why I won't go to dinner with you," she answered honestly. "I'm no longer seeing him."

Lucas's gaze shot to hers and he studied her so long that she found her feet wanting to shuffle beneath the weight of his stare. Instead, she found the strength to step away from him.

"I'm going to check on Cassie."

"I'll be there when I've finished my chart notes on Jenny."

"Take your time." Maybe she'd be finished and not have to see him again.

* * *

"Are you going to go out with Dr. Cain tonight, since you and Richard are history?" Did Meghan have listening devices hidden in the patient rooms or what?

"No, I'm not going out with Dr. Cain. We had our auction date. Tonight, I'm going to stay home and cook."

Meghan wrinkled her nose. "You're crazy, you know."

"I enjoy cooking."

"You could go to the movies with Amy and me."

"No, thank you. I'm cooking because I want to."

To keep her mind occupied she'd enrolled in cooking lessons not long after her divorce was final. Yes, she'd burned more than a few meals prior to figuring out what she was doing wrong, but she had learned. Excelled even. Cooking had been great therapy. Mainly, she'd discovered, as long as she didn't get lost daydreaming about Lucas, her meals had turned out decent. Decent had gone to good. Something she'd detested had gone to something she enjoyed and found therapeutic. As time passed, she'd quit dreaming about Lucas altogether.

Emily left the nurses' station and checked on her patients. Lucas stopped her just outside Jenny's room.

"Are you really going to cook your dinner tonight?"

He sounded so incredulous that she winced. Okay, so she hadn't been able to cook when they got married. That wasn't a sin. There had been lots of things she could do. She'd just grown up in a house where the majority of meals had been takeout and she'd never mastered much more in the kitchen than use of a microwave.

"I can cook." She glared at him, hoping no one was in the hospital hallway to see them, but afraid to look around to check. "I'm not a stagnant person, you know."

"I didn't think you were."

"Then you shouldn't sound so surprised that I've learned to do things I couldn't do so well a few years ago."

"You always were a quick learner." He didn't say more, didn't say to what he referred. He didn't have to.

Emily's brain went there anyway.

Or maybe it wasn't her brain, but her body.

Her body seemed unable to not go there when Lucas was near.

"Prove it."

"Prove what?" she asked, not following him.

"That you can cook."

"I know what you're trying to do. You're just trying to get me to invite you to dinner."

"You're right. That is what I'm trying to do. What are we having?"

"Chopped liver," she said without thought, hating that he was once again keeping pace beside her.

"Chopped liver?"

She almost let a laugh escape from her lips. Almost.

"Oh, yeah." She knew he didn't like liver, that he hated it. "Plus broccoli."

"I see you remember all my favorites."

Glancing toward him, she smiled sweetly. "But of course."

He stared at her a minute, then surprised her by the easy smile that slid onto his face. "I'll come hungry."

"I didn't invite you to dinner," she reminded him.

"But you're going to because you want to prove to me what a great cook you are now."

He had her there. She narrowed her gaze at him in dislike. She did want to impress him with the fact that she wasn't the same person she'd been five years ago. Stupid pride.

"I'm eating at nine. I'll eat without you if you're late."

# CHAPTER SIX

LUCAS COULDN'T SAY the smells that greeted him were the best he'd ever smelled, but they weren't bad.

Immediately after letting him into her apartment, Emily disappeared. She didn't tell him to make himself at home, just opened the door, motioned him in without a smile or a look that said she was glad he was there, then disappeared.

He assumed to the kitchen.

She probably wasn't glad he was there. He'd practically begged for the invitation. Something he didn't quite understand. He'd only wanted to make peace with Emily, to be able to function at the hospital without undue awkwardness between them. Now he wanted to be with her because he liked being with her. Which wasn't in his plans at all, but that didn't seem to have stopped him from pushing for an invite to taste her cooking.

Or from feeling ecstatic that she and the pharmacist were history.

He closed the apartment door behind him and checked out her living room. The comfortably decorated room was a far cry from the hovel where they'd lived when they'd been married. It had taken everything she'd made for them to scrape by.

He'd looked at things differently than she had. He'd been in school, not some lazy bum seeking handouts from his family. Sure, his family hadn't been pleased that he'd married Emily, but they'd never cut off his funds. Plus, he'd had his own money from his trust his grandparents had left him. Maybe he'd taken that for granted. But the reality was, the money had been his and there'd been no reason for him and Emily to struggle financially.

Only, Emily had insisted she made more than enough for them to get by and had refused any help. He'd given in, for the most part, because he'd thought she'd eventually see sense. She hadn't and he'd resented the change she'd imposed upon him.

Or, more likely, he'd hated that she'd been the one supporting them financially. He'd wanted to take care of her, but she'd refused to let him help to the point of being unreasonable, in his opinion.

All because his parents had accused her of being after his money and she'd been determined to prove them wrong, even if it had meant cutting off her nose to spite her face.

How much had the stress of carrying the financial load played into her depression?

He walked over to a shelf, picked up a photo of her parents. He wasn't sure how old the photo was, but they looked exactly the way he remembered. Then again, just because it seemed as if it had been forever since he and Emily had been married, really it hadn't been that long ago.

Five years since a judge had decreed their divorce final.

His hand shook as he set the frame back onto the shelf.

Her living room color pattern was very neutral, very pleasing to the eye. Creams, earth tones, with a few jewel-toned throw pillows tossed on the sofa. She had a few knickknacks scattered about the room, but overall it was a clutter-free look.

Without one trace of her former life.

Not that he'd expected there to be. Just that he noted there wasn't.

Then again, did his own living quarters boast anything of his life with Emily?

No. At least, they hadn't before a few weeks ago when he'd dug out a box of things he'd been unable to bring himself to throw away. Inside the box had been a photo-booth strip they'd had taken in Atlantic City on their one and only trip there. They'd labeled the weekend as their honeymoon.

He'd wanted to take her on a real honeymoon, somewhere exotic, but instead they'd stayed in a cheap budget motel, eaten junk food, lain around on the beach, played in the water, ridden rides and had sex as if they'd been in heat.

Not the honeymoon he'd wanted to give her or that he'd ever imagined, but he could recall few times in his life he'd been happier. When Emily had been happier.

Once upon a time, being with him had made her happy.

His stomach clenched at the memories.

Tired of being in the living room by himself, he followed his nose to where he'd find Emily. The apartment wasn't very big, so it was easy to find where she stood at a stove.

She still wore her apron, but that was where her resemblance to a fifties housewife ended.

Her hair was pulled up high on her head with a few loose tendrils that hung past her shoulders. Her makeup was subtle but perfectly accented her big green eyes, high cheekbones and pouty, all-too-kissable pale pink lips. Beneath the apron was a pair of jeans that showed off long, slender legs and a T-shirt that matched her eyes. All she needed was a television crew filming her and she'd be a cooking show megastar.

He'd certainly tune in week after week to see what new concoction she'd dreamed up.

"It's almost done," she told him, picking up a glass of wine and dumping its contents over a dish on the stove top. "I was just finishing."

"You didn't have to go to any trouble. I really wouldn't have minded takeout."

"I cooked for me, not you."

He glanced around the small but efficient room. A vase with a few colorful flowers sat in the middle of a table. Two expensive-looking plates with ringed napkins in the center and perfectly laid out silverware to the sides sat opposite each other. He'd have bet money she couldn't properly set a table back when they'd been married. Had she looked up how to on the internet or was this another newly acquired skill?

"What are we having?" he asked, eyeing what she was doing. "Liver, broccoli, asparagus and peas?"

"You always were a good guesser." Her eyes twinkled with merriment.

"That's a lot of greens."

"You're a doctor," she reminded him with a sugary sweet fake smile. "I figured you liked eating healthy. Greens are good for you. If you'll have a seat—" she gestured to the round table that sat four "—I'll serve dinner."

Something about the idea of sitting at her table with her waiting on him struck him as wrong. "I don't want you to serve me, Emily."

"It's no problem. You're my guest."

Reluctantly, he sat down in the indicated chair and watched as she picked up his plate and piled on large portions of each dish, put a sprig of green to the side of the meat and set it before him.

She then prepared the second plate, a much less full one, and put it on the table opposite where he sat. "Can I get you something to drink?"

"I should have brought us a bottle of wine." He hadn't brought anything. No wine. No flowers. No anything. He hadn't been thinking. Not about anything but the person's company he wanted. Emily's.

"It's just as well you didn't," she assured him. "I have no desire to drink something that lowers my inhibitions and makes me not think as clearly."

"Especially around me?"

"Lowering my inhibitions was never something you had a problem with."

"You said no that first night and quite a few after."

"Barely." She laughed, a low sound that was more self-derision than humor.

He regarded her for long moments. She didn't look at him but stared at her plate. Her cheekbones had the slightest bit of blush on them, accenting their height and the beauty of her face. When her gaze lifted to his, the intense color of her green eyes beneath darkly fringed lashes stole his breath.

"You want me to tell you I'm sorry I wanted you so much?"

"I don't want you to tell me anything." Her voice was too calm. "I just want you to eat your food."

"Fair enough," he agreed, wondering at the ache that had settled deep into his gut when he'd yet to even take a bite of her specially prepared meal. "Let's talk about work, then. What's your favorite thing about Children's?"

"The kids." She forked a piece of meat, liver no doubt, and popped it into her mouth. "Mmm, that's good."

Lucas would never believe that anyone could make eating liver look sexy. Emily had. Who knew it was even possible?

He picked up his fork, but, rather than take a bite, he toyed with the food. He really didn't like liver. "What about the kids?"

"Everything about them." She gestured to his plate. "Not hungry?"

"Not very."

Her eyes sparkled. "A shame to let good food go to waste."

He agreed. He didn't believe in being wasteful, but he wasn't mentally psyched up to take a bite of liver just yet, either.

So he forked some broccoli and took a tentative bite.

The garlic and butter flavor lightly coating the vegetable surprised him. "This isn't bad."

Her brow arched. "Did you think it would be?"

"Broccoli has never been my favorite dish."

She blinked innocently. "Really?"

"Really." He ate all his broccoli, then eyed the asparagus and liver.

"Sometimes in life we learn to like things we once didn't and vice versa."

"Are we talking about food or how you feel about me?"

"You tell me." She pointed her fork at his plate. "Try the asparagus. It's delicious."

No doubt.

He cut a piece of the long green stalk with his fork. "Here goes."

The butter cream sauce on the asparagus really was delicious. He ate every bite she'd put on his plate.

"Now, for the main dish," she encouraged. "The meat is exquisitely tender and flavored with my own special sauce."

Based on the other two dishes, no doubt he'd have to revise his lifelong claims that he didn't like liver to that he only liked liver prepared by Emily.

She'd taken things he hadn't liked and prepared them in ways that made him reverse his opinion. He could admire that she'd done that. Really, he should applaud the cooking talent she'd acquired since she'd last prepared a meal for him.

Not surprisingly, the meat was as tender as she'd claimed and the flavor was quite good. Not dry and chewy as he remembered his previous trials with liver.

He clapped his hands together. "Bravo."

Her cheeks flushed. "You like it?"

"You meant for me to, right?"

"I suppose."

"Am I going to regret eating this later?" he asked, taking another bite.

"I don't know. Are you?"

"No rat poison or anything that's going to put me in the emergency department?"

"Would you deserve it if there was?"

He had to think about that one for a minute. Mainly because he wondered if she thought he deserved it? Still, despite her quick comeback, he knew she hadn't done anything to him. She wouldn't hurt a fly.

"Maybe I would."

Emily sat quietly eating her food and staring at her plate rather than look at him.

"I'm sorry I hurt you, Emily."

She dropped her fork.

"I'm sorry for a lot of things," he continued, trying not to wince at her pale face. "Especially how sad you became during our marriage. I regret that I ever played any role in you not being happy."

Her gaze lifted to his.

He waited, not trying to hide his sincerity, not surprised at her look of disbelief. Or was that disgust?

She obviously wanted to scream. She practically did. "No. You can't do this to me."

Not understanding her anger, he asked, "What?"

She pushed her plate away from her and shook her head. "You can't come in here apologizing and acting like you regret how we ended."

"I do regret how we ended." More than she'd ever know or believe, he regretted everything that had gone wrong between them. "I've always regretted how we ended."

"Bull." She pushed herself away from the table and

walked over to the refrigerator. She pulled out two individual glass servings of what appeared to be pudding with a dollop of whipped cream on top.

Which didn't exactly fit with the theme of their meal. He loved pudding. Always had.

He had a vague flashback of pushing her away after she'd attempted to make pudding that had turned out to be a clumpy mess instead of anything close to edible.

Not that he'd cared about the pudding, but the broken look in her eyes had about killed him. When she'd started crying yet again, he hadn't been able to stand it, had wanted to take her in his arms and kiss away the tears in her eyes, had wanted to tease her, spread the liquid concoction on her lips and suck it off until they both forgot about everything except each other.

Instead, they'd fought. Badly. He'd stormed out of the house and gone to stay the night at the hospital doctors' lounge. That had been the end.

The night he'd told her if she was that unhappy, she should leave.

She had left. Because she had been that unhappy. He had made her that unhappy.

When he'd come home the next day, she'd been gone and the tiny apartment had never felt more lonely, more claustrophobic, more cheap and distasteful.

He hadn't meant his words. He'd not wanted her to leave. He hadn't wanted her to be unhappy, either. No matter what he'd done, he hadn't been able to make Emily happy.

Pride had taken over and bad had gone to worse.

What an immature idiot he'd been.

A selfish, immature idiot who'd driven away the best woman to ever come into his life. She'd been a likable person. A good person. Honest, wholesome, real, a ray of sunshine on a cloudy day.

A person unlike any he'd ever known.

"I really am sorry things turned out the way they did, Emily. I'm also sorry if that truth upsets you."

"I'm not upset," she obviously lied. Not looking at him, she shrugged. "Life turned out the way it was supposed to."

"Do you believe that?" Because he wasn't so sure. Instead, he wondered if the way they'd ended had left them both with too many unresolved emotions to really ever move on. Then again, perhaps it was only him who felt that way. Maybe she really was happy now and he should just leave well enough alone. So why couldn't he?

"Yes, I do."

"I'm not so sure," he admitted, surprising himself at his honesty, surprising himself by standing and moving to stand near to her.

Emily closed her eyes, bit into her lower lip and felt tortured. Why had Lucas come over to her? Why wasn't he eating his darn pudding?

"Do you remember the first time we kissed?" He bent close and his words seduced her ear, her body, her mind.

Seriously, did he think she'd forgotten their first kiss?

"I do," he continued, so near she could feel the warmth of his breath. "We were standing outside your apartment door and I leaned down to press my lips to yours. Your mouth was the sweetest thing I'd ever tasted and I couldn't get enough. You set me on fire."

Her brain was on fire. So was the rest of her. Hellfire because he was torturing her with past memories. She'd loved him so much, wanted him so much.

But that was long ago.

"What does it matter if I remember?" she asked incredulously, shaking her head. "All of this is crazy. I don't understand why you wanted to eat at my house, because we both know it wasn't so you could try my cooking."

"Your cooking was great," he assured her, still close to

her, too close. "I want the friendship we shared, Emily, before everything went wrong between us. I want to kiss you again. I want to do a lot more than just kiss you. I want all the good there was between us without the golden rings of death to choke out that goodness."

What was he saying? That he wanted them to be friends with benefits? Was he asking her to be his friend while calling their marriage "golden rings of death"? He really was crazy.

"You want to be my friend?" she quipped, her brain still reeling at what he was saying. At the fact that he'd just said he wanted to kiss her again. That he wanted to do more than just kiss her. Darn him. She didn't want to think about Lucas kissing her, doing more than just kissing her.

He was so close, he could kiss her.

The thought had her wanting to back away from him. The thought had her wanting to turn to him and satisfy her curiosity. Had Lucas really kissed the way she recalled him kissing her or did her mind play tricks on her?

"Have you lost all your other friends?"

His lips curved upward in a wry grin. "You know better than that, Emily. I'm a good friend. A very good friend."

Perhaps he had been to his other friends. Not to her. To her, he'd been a mostly absent friend. Although, he probably meant sexual friends.

"Sex?" She rolled her eyes and moved away from him, sitting down at the table and picking up her pudding. "That's what all this is about? Why you outbid Richard? Why you are interfering in my life when I can't stand you? Because you want sex?"

"I told you, I didn't intentionally go to the auction to bid on you. And if the idiot who let me win your bid wasn't willing to fight harder for you, then good riddance. He didn't deserve you, either." He followed her lead and sat back down at the table, too. But rather than pick up his pud-

ding, he leaned toward her. "I don't believe you can't stand
me. I think you want me. Sex was very good between us."

Her lips twisted with bitterness. "Did you think so? I
got the impression you bored of sex with me very quickly."

"Never."

"Then you have very different memories from mine."

That seemed to throw him. He stared at her a moment,
then took a spoonful of his pudding and closed his mouth
around it. "This is good."

"Of course."

Her sarcasm wasn't lost on him and he arched a brow
in question.

"You changed the subject," she accused.

"You want to talk about my memories of sex between
us?"

No. Yes. Maybe. Depended on what he would say.

"Let me tell you. I remember a woman I couldn't get
enough of whom I married and still couldn't get enough
of. A woman whom I was so obsessed with that I wanted
to be with her rather than doing all the things I needed to
be doing, like studying and preparing for my next day's
patients, or doing the things my parents needed of me. A
woman I'd rather spend time with than sleep or eat or anything else."

The blood drained from her face and she felt cold all
over. "I never asked you to put me before anything. I knew
you had to study."

"Saying that and living it are two different things. You
expected me to be the husband you thought I should be.
You cried all the time, Emily. No matter what I did, I felt
I never could do enough, could never make your sadness
that you'd married me go away. Knowing how unhappy you
were made me miserable, too."

"You regretted marrying me from the moment we said
I do."

He didn't immediately deny her claim.

"It's true, isn't it?" Her voice broke as she pushed for a response. She closed her eyes, shook her head. "Allowing you to come here was a mistake."

"I asked myself a dozen times why you did. Why you and the pharmacist are no longer together. Reality is we needed to talk, Emily."

Restlessness hit her and she couldn't stay seated in her chair a moment longer. She jumped up and moved across the kitchen.

"Despite our past and the way things ended, you're as curious as I am to see if the heat is still there. You want to know if you'll melt at my fingertips if I touch you."

"No." She grabbed hold of the countertop and white-knuckled the edges. She didn't want to know those things. Not really. She just… Oh, help her. Curiosity was going to kill her.

"You could have said no to cooking for me," he reminded. "Why didn't you?"

Why had she agreed to let him come to her apartment? Had she just wanted to see him? To spend time with him?

She let go of the countertop, turned away from him.

He stepped over to her, put his hands on her shoulders. "Upsetting you isn't what I want. What I want is to make you feel good, to make you happy. It's what I always wanted but could never seem to get quite right."

# CHAPTER SEVEN

LUCAS WAS TOUCHING her again. Emily didn't want him touching her. The heat of his hands burned right through her T-shirt, scorching her flesh, branding her with memories.

"Why are you saying these things?" she asked, hating that her voice cracked, that she wasn't strong enough to hide her emotions.

His thumbs stroked over her flesh, making tiny waves of awareness shoot through her. "I'm not over you."

Something inside Emily shattered. She wasn't sure if it was her resolve or if it was the glued-back-together pieces of her heart. Either way the impact left her unsteady.

Oh, the times she'd dreamed of this conversation. At times, she'd dreamed of falling into his arms, of their kissing, making love, laughing that they'd ever let anything come between them and vowing to never lose sight of each other again. At others, she'd lift her chin and scornfully laugh at his admission, telling him that ship had long ago sailed.

Instead of doing either, she seemed frozen in place, stiff and cold in his heated hands.

"Emily, when I told you I wanted to be your friend, to kiss you, I was serious." He sounded serious. His hands gently squeezing her shoulders, turning her around to face him, felt serious. "That is what I want. I want to be a part of your life again, to have you be a part of my life. I didn't know that when I took the position at Children's, but I do now."

"What about what I want?" she asked, trying and failing to keep the pain out of her voice. She did not want to give this man any power over her. Feeling pain was letting him have power over her. He didn't deserve that power. He didn't deserve anything from her.

"What do you want, Emily?"

"That one's easy." There went her chin jutting forward. "For you to go away and to never have to see you again."

Silence.

"Is that really what you want?" He touched her chin, forcing her to face him, stared down into her eyes. His gaze searched hers with an intensity that made her legs no sturdier than the barely touched pudding sitting on the table. "Do you want me to resign from my position at Children's, to disappear from your life and never bother you again? Because if that will make you happy, then I'll give you that, Emily. Tell me what you want right now, and I'll do anything within my power to give you what you want."

She blinked up at him, unable to answer with words.

Because the words that would come out weren't the words that should come out.

She wanted him to disappear and never bother her again. Really, she did. That was the absolute best thing that could happen. She'd loved him more than anything in the world and he'd broken her to bits, left her devastated and alone when she'd fallen apart and lost everything. She should hate him.

"Answer me, Emily. Do you want me to go away and never bother you again? To leave Children's and never purposefully cross your path again? Just say the words, and I'll go."

"I…" She paused, her gaze dropping to his mouth. When

had he gotten so close that his breath fanned her lips? When had his warm body become almost flush with hers?

"I don't want to go, Emily, but if that's what you want, I will."

She looked back up, met his cloudy gaze and opened her mouth to answer him, to tell him that, yes, she wanted him to go away, to never bother her again, to leave Children's and to never purposefully cross her path again. She did want all those things.

But none of that came out and whatever she'd been going to say was lost to the pressure of his mouth covering hers in a kiss.

A kiss she didn't want.

A kiss she wanted more than anything else in the whole world.

A kiss that was surprisingly gentle, almost as if he hadn't been able to not kiss her and wasn't completely sure she wouldn't push him away. His lips were soft against hers and somewhere in her mind she recognized that if she told him to stop, he would, that if she pushed him away, he'd let her. That for the moment he was giving her the power, the control, and she could do with it what she would.

Why wasn't she stopping him?

Instead, her body betrayed her, tingling all over, craving to be closer and closer to him.

This was Lucas. Her Lucas. His lips. His hands. His body. Lucas.

She was kissing her ex-husband and the world was still standing around her. Was it perhaps snowing in hell? Or perhaps pigs had learned to fly? All three seemed just as unlikely phenomena.

She needed to push him away.

But she wasn't.

She couldn't.

She needed to tell him to stop.

But she didn't. Couldn't.

She needed to not enjoy the pressure of his lips, the possessive thrusting of his tongue into her mouth.

But she did.

Oh, how she did.

Kissing Lucas had always caused hot lava to fill every inch of her.

He'd been right. She had been curious as to whether or not he could still cause her body to implode with pleasure with the slightest effort on his part.

Her fingers found their way to his nape. His hands had found their way to her bottom and were pressing her hard against his body.

His hard body.

How had that happened so fast?

She squirmed in remembered pleasure. He'd felt so good, made her feel so good physically. So completely and thoroughly satisfied. She craved that satisfaction, that ultimate pleasure that having him inside her had given so many times in the past.

Her head fell back and he trailed kisses down her throat, sucking gently at her skin.

"You feel so good."

She did feel good. She felt good that he was kissing her, touching her. That he wanted her.

But those weren't things that should be making her feel good. He was her ex-husband. They were no longer married, were no longer anything to each other except for painful memories.

So why wasn't she stopping him?

Because sex with Richard hadn't achieved more than a meager orgasm and she wondered if she'd imagined the mind-blowing meltdowns she'd had at the ministrations of this man's mouth, hands and body.

She hadn't imagined a thing. Just Lucas's kisses, his

hands, had her on the brink of volcanic eruption. She wanted that explosion, that release, even if it wasn't real.

She wanted him for an orgasm. The kind that made her want to wrap her legs around his waist and cling as tightly to his body as she could as wave after wave of pleasure shook her.

She'd let him give the pleasure she knew was his to give. She'd take his kisses, his touches, his body inside hers. She'd demand he give her more and more until he lost control and they both saw stars.

This time she was under no illusions of grandeur or love or happily-ever-after.

Lucas cupped Emily's bottom and molded her against where he throbbed. His lips tasted the sweetness of her throat, his tongue nipped into the groove of her collarbone.

She wiggled, grinding her body against his, and he almost swore.

He'd had sex since their divorce. Not once had he felt this heat, this burning. Not even at the pinnacle. They'd not even removed a single item of clothing and he was bursting at the seams. For Emily.

His Emily.

With her, the burn had been about so much more. It had been a heated look, a light stroke of her finger across his skin, an accidental bump of her body against his, and he'd lose focus of everything except taking them both so high they'd never fall back to the ground.

But they had fallen back to the ground and it had been a rough fall. One that had left Emily in constant tears and him feeling helpless to dry them.

He pulled back, cupped her face and made her look at him. "We have to stop."

Her eyes widened, then filled with anger. "No. You are

not going to do this to me. You aren't going to be the one to push me away. Not this time."

The second she'd spat the words at him, regret had filled her face. She'd revealed things she hadn't wanted him to see. Things he suddenly needed to see, to understand.

"What do you mean?" He hadn't pushed her away. He'd wanted her. Always. He'd just not been able to bear the sadness he'd caused her.

"Never mind." She went to pull away, but he held her to him.

"No. I'm not leaving until you tell me."

Her body stiffened, but she didn't fight to get loose. "Then you'd best pull up a chair and make yourself comfortable, because you're in for a long wait."

Why did he feel as if he'd handled this all wrong? Maybe he was destined to always do things wrong with Emily, to always upset her and make her unhappy. Yet she was the only woman he'd ever wanted to do things right with.

"Emily, I want you."

She laughed, but it was a humorless sound that could have just as easily come from a wounded animal who'd just been kicked. "Yes, I can tell by you saying we have to stop after making me think you wanted to have sex with me."

"I do want to have sex with you."

"Would you please make up your mind? Your indecisiveness is killing me."

"I'm not being indecisive. I'm trying to do the right thing."

"Toying with my emotions by seducing me with your kiss, then pushing me away, that's your idea of doing the right thing? You really are a sick one, aren't you?"

He raked his fingers through his hair. "I guess you might see it that way, but hear me out."

"I'm all ears."

"There is nothing better I'd like to do than push you up

onto that countertop and kiss you until you scream with pleasure." His hands dropped to her waist, caressed her there, as if he considered making good on his suggestion.

"But?"

"But I didn't come here for sex, Emily. I came here tonight because I wanted to be with you, because the thought of eating alone, or even with someone else, when I could be with you just wasn't acceptable. I'm here tonight because I needed your company and no one else's would do." His hands moved to her hips, pulled her flush against his hard body and worked her shirt free from her pants. "No one else has ever done. Just you."

His words were aphrodisiacs to her tortured mind and body.

"Maybe we should have just stuck with sex the first time around," she said, arching her pelvis against him and running her fingers along his shoulders.

"Maybe. Certainly, I don't want marriage again." His hands slid beneath her shirt, lighting fires in the wake of his fingers trailing over her skin. "That isn't in my future."

"You think I want marriage to a selfish jerk like you again? Wrong."

Had she really just tugged his shirt out of his waistband while calling him a selfish jerk? Was she really going for his belt?

"You're sure this is what you want?"

She got his belt buckle loose, undid the snap of his pants, his zipper. "What do you think?"

He groaned as her hands flattened against his abdomen, then moved to his hips and pushed downward on his pants. "I'll make it good for you," he promised.

"You better." He always had. From the very first time, he'd made sure she enjoyed what was happening between them.

She always had.

* * *

Emily's breath came in short, hard pants. Her heart raced. Her body was coated in a glistening sweat.

She remembered exactly why she'd allowed to happen what she'd just allowed to happen.

Sex. Good sex. Great sex. Out-of-this-world sex.

If anything, Lucas had been even better than she remembered.

He'd stripped her of her pants, her shirt, kissed every inch of her body, lingering in key places until she'd begged him for more, done her on the counter, on the kitchen table, hard against her refrigerator until they'd both orgasmed. She was pretty sure they'd permanently dented the stainless-steel door.

Now she was a sweaty mess. Naked. And wondered what she'd done.

As much as she probably should, she didn't regret having sex with Lucas.

If anything, she wanted to thank him.

She'd thought she'd lost the ability to do the things her body had just done.

She hadn't. No way, she hadn't. With Lucas, she'd felt like a sex goddess, like the queen of phenomenal sex, like a fiery siren who gave as good as she got.

"Thank you," Lucas breathed into the curve of her neck. "Thank you, Emily."

"No." She shook her head and began separating her body from his. "Thank you."

She picked up her clothes from the various places they'd landed in their fevered removal, but she didn't rush to redress. She didn't want him to think she was self-conscious in front of him. She wasn't. He'd seen her naked and flushed with the afterglow of sex many times before.

She'd just had sex for the sake of sex and for no other reason. Should she feel guilty or cheap?

"You were amazing."

She flicked her gaze his way. He was smiling, looking arrogant and proud and satisfied. She'd done that. She'd put that look on his face, had given as good as she'd gotten. She knew she had, that he'd been right there with her all the way right up until they'd climaxed in a loud, guttural cry.

"So were you," she admitted, starting to feel claustrophobic as the implications of what they'd done hit her. They'd just had unprotected sex.

What had she been thinking?

What had he been thinking?

Obviously neither of them had been thinking.

Panic built within her chest. So much so that she needed him gone, needed time to think, to process what had happened between them. She was on the pill, but what if something went wrong and she got pregnant?

She couldn't. She just couldn't. What if…?

"I need you to leave while I go take a shower." Even to her own ears her voice sounded panicked, high-pitched.

Confusion replacing the satisfaction on his face, his brows veed together. "Huh?"

"I'm going to take a shower." She tried to sound calm. She didn't want him to know how shaken she was by their having had sex. By the fact that, since Lucas didn't know she was on oral contraceptives, he had just risked getting her pregnant, something he'd meticulously made sure to never risk while they'd been married.

She met his gaze and didn't so much as blink as she stared him down. She couldn't or the tears she was fighting might spill free. "Be gone from my apartment when I get out of the shower."

# CHAPTER EIGHT

CASSIE BELLOWS'S NIGHT NURSE reported that the child had cried in pain most of the night. They'd given her medication, but even in her sleep tears had fallen.

Emily's heart twisted as she took report on the little girl. She hated the thought of the child in so much pain that she'd cried even during sleep.

"I called Dr. Cain and he'll be by this morning to check on her. He plans to get her into surgery this week."

Lucas was coming by.

Of course he was coming by. He worked there. She worked there. They'd see each other, behave professionally as if they hadn't had sweaty kitchen sex the night before, and they'd be polite.

Only, when Lucas came in, he wasn't polite. He was irritated. With her.

He should be grateful that she wasn't a wide-eyed innocent who wanted marriage, children and happily-ever-after as she'd been when they first met.

Children. Emily's breath caught and for a moment a wave of dizziness almost overtook her. Why hadn't Lucas mentioned birth control the night before? Why hadn't she thought to ask him? Why hadn't he worn a condom? He was a wealthy man, one whose parents had accused her of trying to trap him.

If only they knew the truth. If only Lucas knew.

"When was Cassie's last dose of painkiller?" he practically growled.

Emily leaned in and pointed to the computer screen.

"Right there." She tapped the screen, pulling up where the medication was recorded. He was still fairly new. Maybe he truly hadn't known. Then again, Lucas was a quick study. She would guess he knew more ins and outs of their computer system than she did after being there for years.

He studied the screen, then frowned. "I want to increase her dose." He named the quantity.

She made a mental note. "With her next dose due when?"

"Now. Give the medication," he ordered. "I don't want Cassie in pain. I'm taking her to surgery early in the morning. Even if she stays sedated most of the day, that's preferable to her crying in constant pain. I'd do surgery today if I could have gotten an operating suite and team approved." His look said he wasn't very happy that he'd been unable to. Perhaps that was why he'd been irritable when he'd joined her.

"Cassie's status changed a great deal overnight."

Looking stressed, he nodded. "As much as I hate to expose her to more imaging, I've requested an MRI brain scan that I want done stat. Whether they want to approve it or not, the operating room staff may have to find me a suite and staff today."

Part of her couldn't believe she was having a normal work conversation with the man she'd had crazy hot sex with the night before. Then again, they'd had normal conversations after having phenomenal sex in the past. So why it seemed odd to her now she wasn't sure, just that it did.

"About last night," he began, and she cringed. So much for her previous thoughts.

She shook her head. "You don't need to worry. I'm on birth control, so let's not have this conversation. Especially not at work."

The fatigue etched on his face earlier returned. "That's not what I wanted to talk about, although it probably should have been. Still, you're right. This isn't the time or place."

"Agreed." As far as she was concerned, there never would be a time or place for that conversation.

She'd rather chalk that one up to rebound sex or curiosity sex or just "spur of the moment because Lucas was hot" sex.

Right or wrong, this time she'd keep her head high rather than drowning in a thousand pitiful tears.

Sure, she'd had a moment of questioning herself when she'd walked into her kitchen, prepared to straighten up the mess from their meal only to find he'd already done so. She'd done the majority while she'd been cooking their meal, but he'd loaded their dishes into the dishwasher, wiped down the countertops and table, and her kitchen had looked as if he'd never been there.

"I'd ask you to dinner so we could talk about last night," he interrupted her thoughts, "but I may be tied up in the operating room."

"You really think something emergent has happened?" She wasn't going to bother to acknowledge how his comment affected her heart rate or her pretense of calm. Nor would she tell him that she thought their seeing each other again outside of work was a bad idea.

"With the changes in her vitals and pain level? It'll surprise me if her test doesn't come back showing something different."

"What do you suspect?" After all, the brain tumor had been there for months and months with only gradual changes in her neurological status. Cassie's condition shouldn't have changed so drastically from her tumor.

"If I didn't know better, I'd suspect a bleed. But the tumor shouldn't have caused that. She's fallen several times prior to her admission, but she's had imaging that didn't show any evidence of a bleed or fluid buildup." His words seemed to be brainstorming as much as telling her his thoughts.

As much as she didn't want to share any kind of connection to him, she liked the insight to how his mind worked, liked that she could tell he was open to any ideas she might have.

"A bleed seems the most logical explanation for a sudden change," she agreed.

"I need to get the kid into surgery, get that tumor out and find out what the unknown is."

She recalled his talking about unknowns in the past. There were the known unknowns and the unknown unknowns and the latter were the ones that in his profession were the killers. Hearing him say the word swamped her with a wave of nostalgia that she quickly shoved aside.

No more nostalgia allowed. None. Only...

She stared at him a few minutes, at the concern on his face. He sincerely cared about Cassie and her outcome.

Not that he was an uncaring person, but when he'd been in medical school, he'd seemed removed from his patients, more as if they were just case studies and diagnoses, not real people. It had struck her when she'd walked in on him doing the puzzle with Cassie. Never in the past could she have imagined him working on a puzzle with a child. Now he fretted over what was going on beneath the surface with the girl's health. He was worried about what her unknown was.

He cared. He truly cared about his patient.

The same as he cared about Jenny and had looked so protective of the child. Emily had liked that look. Which she didn't like. Because the less she liked about Lucas, the better.

They'd had their shot, hadn't worked, and the things that had torn them apart were all still there. They weren't meant to be and to let herself get caught up in the spell just being near him again wove would only lead to heartache for her.

She didn't want to think Lucas had a soft side. A vulnerable, caring side.

It was much easier to think of him as the one who'd given up on their marriage and no longer wanted her. The one who hadn't had a heart.

If she saw him as a person with a heart, didn't that mean she had to wonder what it had been about her that had caused him to push her away?

Lucas had known. Of course, in this one instance, he wished he'd been wrong.

Then again, at least seeing the pocket of fluid on Cassie's brain explained why his functioning patient from the day before had gotten into serious trouble overnight. Most likely she had a slow hemorrhage from one of her falls related to her poor balance. The poor kid couldn't seem to get a break.

He scrubbed his hands, gloved up and proceeded to the operating table where Cassie Bellows was anesthetized.

Sometimes, it still awed him that he was a brain surgeon. Him. A spoiled rich kid who'd never had any real responsibilities until he got to medical school.

Once there, he'd done just fine except for the short period of time he'd been with Emily. During that time, he'd had a neurosurgeon mentor pull him aside and tell him he'd best get his act together or he was going to make a mistake that could be detrimental to his patients' lives and Lucas's career.

One thing he'd always known was that he didn't want to follow in his financial guru father's wealthy footsteps. He'd wanted to follow his own path and life calling, to make a positive difference in the world. When in high school a classmate had suffered TBI from a football injury, Lucas had become fascinated with the boy's care and known that was what he wanted to do with his life. Perhaps living off his parents' money while achieving that hadn't been making his own way in many people's eyes, but, until Emily, Lucas had never questioned his right to do so. It was what he'd grown up expected to do.

Emily had made him feel guilty for living an easy life. Wasn't that what his parents wanted for him? What they'd worked to give him? Should he have refused their help, left his trust funds untouched and struggled? What purpose would that have served? He was an only child, his parents loved him, and they'd not understood Emily's aversion to their help, especially since they'd been so suspicious of her motives. Still, other than with educational expenses, he'd abided by the rules Emily had set about taking money from his parents.

He still didn't agree with Emily, but time had given him the ability to at least have a better understanding. Perhaps she'd wanted him to have a better understanding of who she was, of where she'd come from, to where they had more insight into each other's world.

Either way, it had been his inability to juggle a depressed new wife along with his other obligations that had been the big problem, not his parents' money.

He'd tried to stop Emily's tears but had only seemed to make them worse. Being around her, knowing he'd caused her unhappiness, had left him feeling impotent. When he'd catch glimpses of her at the hospital, she seemed fine. Only around him did the waterworks start. So he'd stayed away more and more, focused on the things he had control over and hoped his wife would kick out of her depression.

Instead, she had started talking babies almost nonstop.

He'd full out panicked. What little time he'd had away from studies, he'd spent away from her and the longing he could see in her eyes for something he simply couldn't give her. Not at that point in their marriage, which was something she hadn't seemed to understand or accept. He knew people managed a lot more than what had been on his plate, but, for him, he'd already felt he was halfway doing too many things.

What if her depression had gotten worse? What if she hadn't been able to deal with a baby and he'd had to take on that load, too? He'd have made it work, but he'd worried about the effects on Emily. Which had affected him. Affected them. They'd grown further apart. He'd wanted to make Emily happy, had tried to. Instead, she'd gone into deeper despair and refused to seek help.

He'd failed on all counts.

Here he was scrubbing up for surgery and distracted from what he was doing by memories from the past. He needed to put Emily out of his head. Far, far out of his head until he finished with Cassie's surgery.

Which proved a little more difficult than he would have thought when he walked into the surgical suite. Despite the fact he could see only her green eyes beneath her surgical gear, he immediately recognized her. Emily was in the operating room.

What was she doing there and why?

Emily had started out in the operating room at Children's. It had been the only job opening when she'd applied. She'd been desperate to escape working with Lucas every day and had taken the first offer that had presented itself.

Which made her recognize the irony of her volunteering to go into the operating room with him this evening. Truly, she'd come full circle.

She'd had only an hour left on her shift. The hospital had been scrambling to put together a team for the operating room, and before she'd been able to give better thought to it, she'd volunteered to work overtime and assist.

Since Jenny had remained stable, and Cassie was her only other patient, getting the okay for Emily to go into the surgical suite had been an easy process and one the hospital had appreciated her doing.

Now that she was here, watching Lucas drill a hole into the child's skull, she wondered if she'd been too hasty.

As gruesome as some of the surgeries she'd assisted in were, that aspect didn't bother Emily. She knew what they were doing was to Cassie's benefit and without the procedure the child's odds of survival were poor.

If she did survive, the longer surgery was delayed, the higher the risk of permanent brain damage.

It was watching the precision and expertise with which Lucas worked that was getting to her. Her gaze kept wandering to him.

She performed her job duties with remembered ease, always there to hand him what he needed, to assist in any way, along with the others assisting with the procedure.

When Lucas located the tiny hemorrhage that was causing so many problems, when he got the bleed stopped, he sighed in relief. He looked up, sought her gaze, and although she couldn't see more than his eyes, she saw so much.

The relief, the fear that had been eased. He'd cared about Cassie, cared that he took good care of her. She wasn't a number or a case study. She was a child who'd been assigned to his care. He took that seriously.

Emily was glad.

So glad that she smiled at him. Not that he could see her beneath the mask, but maybe he knew because she'd swear he smiled back even though she couldn't see his mouth beneath the surgical mask, either.

What was happening? She did not want to feel any kind of bond with Lucas. Not physical, not emotional, not professional, not any.

Yet, at this moment, she felt as if time had never passed and she was looking into the eyes of the man who'd stolen her heart rather than the one who'd broken it.

* * *

When her doorbell rang later that night, Emily wasn't surprised by who was on the other side of her viewer despite the late hour.

Nor was she truly surprised by the fact she opened the door to let him in.

"I know it's almost midnight, but…" he said, stepping inside, looking tired and a bit forlorn, as if he wasn't sure he should be there, but that he hadn't been able to stay away.

She understood.

So when he took her in his arms and kissed her, she kissed him right back. Why not? It was just sex. Really, really good, hot sex. Or so she kept telling herself because no way would she let herself consider for even the remotest possibility that she could be falling back under Lucas's spell.

He kissed her, held her, breathed her in as if he was starved for everything about her. She understood. She felt the same.

They made it to her bed, remembering the condom this time, and reached just as high heights as they had the night before. When they'd climaxed and Emily lay there trying to catch her breath, Lucas stroked his fingers over her lower back, tracing the dip right above her buttocks.

He was so good, such a perfect lover. Only, he wasn't her lover. Not really. He was a man she was having sex with whom, if she wasn't careful, she would end up being destroyed by again. She couldn't let herself fall into the trap of thinking they had a second chance. To do that would be foolish and asking for trouble.

Within minutes, his breathing evened out and she realized he'd dozed off. Panic hit her. She rolled over onto her side to face him and shook his shoulders. "You can't go to sleep. You have to leave."

"I know." But he didn't open his eyes.

He'd looked so tired when he'd arrived that she felt guilty. It was long after midnight.

But she couldn't sleep with Lucas. She couldn't snuggle up next to him and close her eyes and drift off into sleep, expecting to wake next to him. For one, what if he was gone when she woke? How devastating would that be? But even more important, what kind of expectations would her heart attach to waking next to Lucas? To sleep next to the man she'd once thought she'd spend the rest of her life sleeping next to, to wake next to the man she'd once given all her love to, was just too intimate. She couldn't do it.

With more gusto, she shook him again. "Lucas, you need to get out of my bed. You can't stay here."

His eyes opened and he frowned.

"Why not? What does it matter?" Lucas asked, yawning as he stretched in her bed and looked way too perfect as the covers slipped low on his waist.

Fighting to keep her gaze trained on his face, she assured him, "It matters."

"Why?"

Why? Such an innocent question, but the answers ran much deeper than she could ever elaborate.

"I don't want you here," she answered as simply as she could. Perhaps a grand oversimplification, but she didn't want him there.

"You wanted me here a few minutes ago," he reminded her, rolling onto his side and grinning sleepily at her.

"That was just sex."

Lord, she hoped what they'd shared was just sex on her part. She couldn't go through another round of heartbreak. She'd barely survived the first time.

*Just sex.* The words rankled Lucas. Just sex. He didn't want anything permanent. So just sex should be fine. So why did her claim irritate him?

What he did want was her friendship back. He'd always been able to talk to her, to share his thoughts, to tell her things that had happened throughout the day. Right up until they'd gotten married, that was. Then their communication skills had gone missing. Eventually, they'd been leading completely separate lives.

How had that happened between him and the woman he'd been so crazy about?

He reached out and ran his fingertip over her bare hip. She was beautiful. Ethereal even. "You're sure you don't want me to stay?"

"Positive." She climbed out of the bed and handed him his underwear to prove her point.

"Have you eaten?"

She nodded. "I heated up something when I got home."

He saw the hesitation on her face, the battle that took place prior to her asking, "Did you?"

He shook his head. "I'm starved."

Her shoulders stiffened and again war waged within her. "There's a twenty-four-hour Chinese takeout that's pretty good on the corner."

Sitting up on the side of the bed, he nodded. He could take a hint. She really did want him to leave.

"Or I could heat up some leftovers from last night."

"Liver, broccoli and asparagus after midnight?"

She nodded.

What was wrong with him that he'd rather eat his three least favorite foods in the early-morning hours than go get Chinese takeout?

"Okay, sounds good." He wasn't lying. The thought of spending more time with her did sound good.

Because he wanted more from Emily than just sex.

He always had wanted more from Emily than just sex.

He wanted her in his life.

Just this time, they wouldn't make the mistake of marriage.

* * *

Why had Emily offered to heat up leftovers for Lucas? She berated herself over and over as she pulled plastic containers from her refrigerator.

She should have made him leave. He was a big boy. He wouldn't have starved. He'd obviously been feeding himself for the past five years just fine without her.

He'd been doing just fine on a lot of things without her.

Because his body was honed to a lean muscle machine. He'd always been fit, but he'd taken his physique to a higher level.

Which she'd thoroughly appreciated when it came to the man's endurance and stamina. He was a truly phenomenal lover.

Not because of his body, although that was certainly easy on the eye. No, it was what he did to her body, how he looked at her as if she were the most desirable thing he'd ever seen, as if he couldn't kiss her, touch her, be inside of her nearly enough if he spent the rest of his life trying. It was in the combination of desperation, awe and tenderness in which he touched her. As if she were precious and he couldn't quite believe he was with her, touching her. Those were the things that made him a phenomenal lover.

He made her feel special.

He had before, too.

Which was how she'd ended up giving him her virginity despite the fact she'd intended to wait until marriage. An outdated view, she knew and openly admitted, but she'd thought it a gift she'd wanted to save for her husband.

She'd been as desperate for consummation as he'd been and they'd never even discussed marriage on the afternoon he'd surprised her by coming by her apartment earlier than expected. She'd been reading a nursing magazine and he'd walked in, kissed her, and even before they'd gone to her bedroom, she'd known she wasn't going to stop him that time as she had before. She'd known she was desperately in love with him and wanted him to be her first even if she'd known he was wildly out of her league.

He'd proposed a month later and they'd married the month after that. Everything had been rushed, but it had been what Lucas had wanted and she'd been so ecstatic that she'd just gone along for the ride.

In hindsight, she realized she should have known better.

They'd been as different as night and day.

"What are you thinking about?"

She spun toward his voice. "Why?"

"Because you've been standing there opening and closing that plastic lid over and over for the past five minutes."

"Oh." But she didn't tell him she'd been thinking about them. She probably didn't have to. After the past two nights, he probably had a pretty good idea what weighed on her mind. "I don't like you, you know."

"That's what you were thinking about?"

"I don't want to date you," she added, ignoring his question.

"Okay." He didn't argue.

"Our having sex again is a very bad idea."

"Probably."

She swapped the bowl in the microwave out for the one she held. "I don't like you."

"You've already said that."

"I just wanted to make sure we were clear."

"Why don't you like me, Emily?"

"Because…" Because he'd broken her heart into a zillion pieces that had never completely fit back together no matter how she'd tried. Because he was so freaking perfect and she was just her. Because… "You're my ex-husband. I'm not supposed to like you."

"Says who?"

"Says everyone."

"Since when did you listen to what everyone says?" he challenged.

"Don't act like you know me. I've changed a lot the past five years."

His gaze skimmed over her from her face down her T-shirt, gym shorts, and then over her legs to her bare feet. It was all she could do to hold her toes still rather than shuffle her feet at his inspection.

"You haven't changed that much."

"Maybe not on the surface, but inside I've changed a lot." The microwave dinged, indicating the bowl was heated, but she didn't remove it, just stared at him, refusing to let her gaze waver. "I'm not an innocent kid anymore that it's easy for some smooth-talking man to come along and take advantage of."

"Is that how you saw me back then? As a smooth-talking man who took advantage of your innocence?"

Did she? Not really. "You were definitely more experienced in the ways of life than I was."

"A rock was more experienced in the ways of life than you were."

She wasn't sure if she should be offended or not.

"Good thing I decided to go out and get a life." She turned, took the bowl out of the microwave, grateful the dish was still warm. "I'll let you take out however much you want. You may need to throw your plate back into the microwave for a few minutes, though."

"Why did you open your apartment door, Emily? For sex?"

Why did he think she'd opened the door?

"We have nothing in common, have no desire to build a future together, no history we want to repeat. The only thing we have between us is good sex. Of course sex is why I opened my apartment door. Now, hurry up and finish your food so you can leave. I'm tired and scheduled to work tomorrow."

Her words sounded so logical, so like she believed them. If only she did. If only when she looked at him she didn't long for things that would never be.

# CHAPTER NINE

CASSIE WAS STILL in a medication-induced coma when Emily took report the following morning. She was grateful the child didn't seem to be in pain or suffering. Her poor mother, on the other hand, was a wreck when Emily checked on the girl.

"When will she wake up?" the woman asked from where she sat next to Cassie's bed.

"That depends on a lot of things. For right now, Dr. Cain believes it's in her best interest to keep her unconscious to give her more time to recover from her procedure."

"She's not going to know anything, is she?"

A scary question, because the increased intracranial pressure from the bleed had only complicated things that were already complicated enough.

"There's really not a way to know at this point. I do know Dr. Cain is very hopeful that she won't have lost any major body function or thought processes."

"She might not know who I am when she wakes up," Mrs. Bellows cried. "Do you know how horrible that will be if my baby wakes up and doesn't know who I am? And this isn't even it. Once she recovers from this, she'll still have to have the tumor removed. Life is so unfair."

Cassie's mother began sobbing. Emily stopped what she was doing and held her, letting her cry on her shoulder.

"Dr. Cain is an excellent neurosurgeon. From everything he said, he views the surgery as a success. Let's wait and see how Cassie is when she wakes up before we borrow trouble," she soothed. "She's going to need you to be strong for her."

Who was she to tell this woman to be strong? She'd never dealt with a child who had to have brain surgery. She'd never gotten to deal with a living, breathing child at all, which wrenched her heart with a grief she rarely let rear its ugly head. Sometimes she felt so inadequate at her job. Sometimes she wished she had the power to instantly heal her patients.

"I know she is going to need me," Cassie's mother agreed. "I want to be strong, but this is hard."

"I can only imagine," she answered honestly. "All Cassie's vitals held during the night and this morning, too. Everything is stable. That's a blessing."

The woman nodded. "I'm just being impatient, wanting her to wake up and be normal."

"Hopefully, that's exactly where she will be soon."

Both women jumped at the voice joining their conversation.

"Dr. Cain."

"Lucas," Emily said at the same time, then corrected herself. "Dr. Cain, we didn't hear you come in."

"I see that." He smiled empathetically at Cassie's mother but didn't look at Emily. "How's our girl this morning?"

"The same as last night when you stopped by about two."

He'd come back to the hospital after leaving her apartment? Did the man sleep? While they'd been married, she'd often wondered how he pulled the long hours he did, how he got by on so little sleep.

"Thank you for that, by the way," Mrs. Bellows continued. "You sitting with me meant a lot."

Not only had he stopped by, but he'd stayed and sat with

Cassie's mother. Why? Seemed she asked that question a lot where Lucas was concerned these days.

She stared at him, taking in his dark navy scrubs that did little to hide his abundant sex appeal. His dark hair was ruffled, whether by the wind or from running his fingers through the silky tufts she wasn't sure.

She'd run her fingers through his hair the night before. She'd… No, she was not going to go there.

What little sleep he'd gotten the night before must have been in the doctors' lounge. Why?

"If there's nothing you need from me, Dr. Cain, I'm going to check on my other patient," Emily said, needing to get away from him, away from her questions.

"Sorry I went all boo-hoo on you," Cassie's mother apologized, rising from her chair and giving Emily a quick hug.

"Not a problem." She hugged the woman tightly, then didn't wait for Lucas to say anything, just exited the room as quickly as she could without causing a commotion.

"What have you been up to? Because you look guilty as sin," Meghan pointed out the moment Emily stepped into the hallway.

With a backward glance toward Cassie's room, she shushed her friend. "Nothing."

"Right. That's why your cheeks are all flushed and your eyes have a light in them that I never saw Richard put there."

"Shh!" she repeated. "I don't have a light in my eyes unless it's tears from how much my heart hurts from what my patient and her family are going through."

"Sorry, I heard about Cassie's brain bleed and how you volunteered as a surgical nurse last night near the end of your shift." Meghan's gaze cut back toward Cassie's room. "He's in there, isn't he?"

"I've no idea where Richard is." She purposely misunderstood. She didn't want to talk about Lucas, not even with Meghan. "I told you we ended things."

"I wasn't referring to your pharmacist and you know it."

Emily sighed. She should have known Meghan wouldn't let her get away with that one. Still, at least she'd bought a few seconds to collect herself a little.

She grabbed her friend's arm and walked her away from Cassie's room. "Yes, I know who you mean, and yes, he is in there, and no, I don't want to talk about him."

An "I knew it" smile spread across Meghan's face. "You had sex with him, didn't you?"

"What?"

Meghan gave her a no-brainer look. "Don't bother denying it, because I know you did. I've never seen you look so twitterpated."

"I am not twitterpated. If that's even a word."

"Sure it's a word. Didn't you ever watch that kids' cartoon with the deer?"

She frowned.

"And you, my friend, are twitterpated."

"If that means I'm aggravated at you for making wild accusations, then yep, I am."

"I note you said wild and not false."

Knowing she was fighting a losing battle, she just shrugged and stared at her friend.

Meghan's mouth dropped open and her eyes sparkled with animation. "You did. You had sex with Dr. Cain. Was he as awesome as he looks like he'd be?"

Would the floor please open up and swallow her now?

"I'm not answering that and would you please whisper? I don't want anyone to overhear you."

"You don't have to answer." Meghan looked as if she might burst with excitement. Seriously, had her friend disliked Richard that much? "I can tell by your face."

Emily glanced around the busy hospital hallway. "This is not where we should be having this conversation."

"Then let's go have dinner together after we get off work this evening. You can tell me everything."

Emily didn't meet her friend's eyes.

"You can't, can you? Because you're seeing him?"

Emily shrugged again. "We don't have any specific plans."

"But you're hoping you'll see him?" Meghan guessed again.

"I suspect I will."

How ridiculous was she being? She was not going to go home and wait around in hopes that Lucas would show up for another round of sex. She just wasn't.

Yet that was exactly what she'd been thinking when she'd not agreed to Meghan's suggestion.

"Let's do it," she said, unwilling to start the "sitting around waiting on him" bit. She'd been there and done that years ago. "Where do you want to meet?"

Meghan arched a brow. "You're sure?"

"Absolutely."

How pathetic was Lucas that he was knocking on Emily's apartment door hoping to be invited back into her bed?

Pretty pathetic.

So why was he still standing there?

Because he was crazy about her.

He hadn't meant to fall for Emily again, but he was hooked. If he hadn't realized before, when she'd thrown him out the previous night he had realized how much he wanted to stay. How much he wanted her to want him to stay.

And not just for sex.

Are you home? he texted, leaning back against her apartment door frame and wondering at his current state of sanity, or lack thereof.

Nope, came her almost instant reply.

She wasn't home. At least she hadn't been ignoring him.

Where are you?

On a date.

On a date? His stomach knotted.

With the pharmacy guy?

Nope. We broke up. This date is a lot hotter.

You're on a date with yourself?

He was trying to tease her into telling him who she was with, trying to curb the jealousy surging through his veins.

Not hardly.

Lucas gripped his phone in his hands a lot tighter than he should. Emily was on a date and was being vague about who she was with. How could she be on a date after having sex with him the night before? The night before that, too?

Then again, he had no claims on her. Just a strong desire to be with her and the inability to stay away.

My date says you should join us.

Lucas blinked at his phone.

Your date wants your ex-husband to join you?

Doesn't know about you. No one does, remember?

How could he forget? She'd completely erased all traces of him from her life. Which he supposed was what he'd done with her, too. Yet he didn't like that their time together had been completely obliterated.

You should tell him, he suggested, trying to squelch his jealousy.

Not a him.

Not a… Why did relief flood him that she wasn't with another man just hours after being with him? Because he wanted her.

All of her.

Just for him.

I'm with Meghan.

The pretty brunette nurse who worked on the pediatric neuro floor who'd been with Emily the night of the fundraiser. He'd seen her around the hospital and always made a point to say hi.

Where are you?

She told him the name of a club a couple blocks away.

I'll be right there.

"He's on his way," Emily stage-whispered to Meghan, leaning across the bar table to give her friend a pleading look. "Now what?"

"Now you get to have some fun with Dr. Yummy Tummy."

"How do you know his tummy is yummy?"

Meghan giggled. "Well, isn't it?"

Yes, Lucas's stomach was pretty yummy. Pretty cut. Pretty six-packed.

She sighed. "I shouldn't have invited him here."

"Why not?"

"Because it's our night."

"Emily, I love you, hun, but you've not been with me since we got here."

"Huh?"

"Don't think I haven't noticed that you've checked your phone every two minutes, and when he finally texted, you almost passed out with relief."

Her shoulders sagging, she squished up her nose. "I did, didn't I?"

Her friend nodded. "So tell me about him. Besides the obvious."

"The obvious?"

"That he's hot and has the hots for you."

"Obviously, I have the hots for him, too," she admitted, wondering at how much she should tell Meghan. She and the woman had instantly hit it off when Emily had started at Children's and their friendship had grown over the years. She loved Meghan, but telling her, telling anyone, about Lucas made her nervous. Still, she needed an objective opinion and there was no one she trusted more than Meghan.

"Obviously." Her friend laughed, taking a sip of her drink.

Emily followed suit, taking a small sip of her diet soda and a huge leap of faith. "I used to be married to him."

"What?" The loud music and dim lights did nothing to hide Meghan's shock.

Emily swirled the contents of her glass. "He's my ex-husband."

Meghan looked floored. "Dr. Cain is your ex-husband? The one you were devastated by when you started at Children's? The one who it took you years to get past and start dating again? That ex-husband?"

Toying with the tiny straw in her drink, Emily nodded. "Yep, he used to be all mine."

Which sounded an awful lot like she wanted him to be all hers again, because, seriously, she could have just said "yes, that ex-husband," right?

She didn't want him to be all hers again. Did she?

She couldn't. To want that would be begging for heartache and tears.

Only…

Meghan let the implications sink in. "Did he know you worked at Children's when he accepted the position?"

"He knew. He said my being there was his only hesitation with accepting."

Meghan's forehead wrinkled. "I don't understand. Why would he buy your date at the auction if you were what made him hesitate on accepting the position?"

"Because he's here to torture me." Okay, so that was an exaggeration, but being near Lucas, kissing him, having sex with him, all of it was torture because she knew it was temporary.

Meghan's brow arched. "Seriously?"

Emily took another sip of her soda. "Actually, I don't really understand why he bought my date. He says he wants for us to get along and not be awkward at work, but he didn't have to win my bid if that's what he wanted. I've never been able to resist him long."

"Maybe he didn't think you'd ever let him close enough without the forced time together."

"Maybe. Regardless, he's close enough now. Too close." What had she done? "Meghan, what am I going to do when we quit having sex?" Quit having sex because, really, she couldn't call it dating. They'd gone out to eat at Stluka's, she'd cooked for him, and they'd had sex twice. That didn't exactly qualify as boyfriend/girlfriend. She didn't want Lucas to be her boyfriend. She'd been there, done that and had the divorce papers to prove it. "The last time he and I got involved, I ended up leaving my job. I love my job at Children's. I'd prefer not to change jobs every time he shows up in my life."

Meghan shrugged. "Then don't change jobs."

If only it were that simple.

"You don't understand what it was like after we split and I had to go to work knowing I'd see glimpses of him there…" Her voice trailed off. She'd dreaded each and every day. Had wondered how he could see her and not know the great loss within her. The grief and suffering she felt every moment of every day and seeing him going on about his life had only added to her pain and loss. She'd quickly known she couldn't continue working there and had turned in her notice. Starting work at Children's had been a godsend.

"I knew you had been married before, but you never wanted to talk about it, so I never asked." Meghan winced, then took a sip of her drink. "I remember how sad you looked when you first started. The first time I ever saw you, I wanted to hug you and beat the crap out of whoever had hurt you."

"Our friendship was formed on pity?"

Meghan shook her head. "Our friendship was formed based upon the person you are being someone I came to love. You're a great friend, Emily."

"Even though I never told you about Lucas?"

"I wish you'd felt you could tell me, but I understand why you didn't, why you wouldn't want to talk about him at all. He hurt you a lot, didn't he?"

Lucas had hurt her a lot, but what had come later had hurt so much more. Still hurt so much. One never got over that kind of hurt, she supposed.

"I guess in some ways we hurt each other."

"Are you sure getting involved with him again is a good idea? I mean, he's superhot and all, but aren't you afraid you'll end up getting hurt again?" Meghan reached across the bar table and touched Emily's hand. "Maybe we should leave before he gets here. I don't want to see you hurt."

She shook her head. "I'm not going to let him hurt me again."

Her friend didn't look convinced. "How are you going to stop him?"

Emily lifted her chin a notch. "Because this time I'm the one in control. I'm the one telling him to leave instead of the other way around."

Meghan blinked. "He told you to leave?"

Unable to give voice to that particular memory, Emily nodded.

Meghan stared at her as if she'd lost her mind.

Possibly, she had. But when her gaze collided with that of the man who was making his way toward their table, she admitted that rational thought didn't matter because she wanted him too much to stop this craziness.

From the moment he'd bought her bachelorette date, her fate had been sealed. Maybe from the moment she'd first met him, her fate had been sealed. Lord knew that even though she'd convinced herself she could be happy and content with a man like Richard, deep down she wondered if she would have been. Would anyone other than the man intently making his way toward her table do?

"He's here."

"You want me to leave?" Meghan offered, suddenly looking nervous.

Emily grabbed her friend's hand. "Please don't. Make me show some restraint, because when I look at that man, I just want to rip his clothes off with my teeth."

Meghan looked toward him and groaned. "Emily, a lot of women want to rip that man's clothes off with their teeth when they look at him. No offense, but he's easy on the eyes to say the least."

He was easy on the eyes. Clothed and unclothed.

She sighed. "What am I going to do?"

"What do you want to do?"

"I've already told you what I want to do. That's the problem."

Meghan grinned, then made a chomping motion.

Emily rolled her eyes but smiled at her friend.

"Why not? Obviously, he's good at what he does. Just so long as you stay in control and remember that he's bad for you regarding anything but physical gratification, why not use him for good sex?"

Why not indeed?

Other than that she'd never been the kind of girl to have sex just for the sake of sex.

Well, not until now.

Now that was exactly what she had been doing, right? No matter what lay in the recesses of her heart, she knew she and Lucas had no future. Yet she'd had sex with him the past two nights. She'd have a torrid affair with her ex-husband, let him rock her world, then she'd send his butt home night after night because to allow him to stay would change the dynamics of their relationship. She'd keep everything neatly within the physical rather than the emotional.

"Hello, Dr. Cain," Meghan greeted as he joined their table. She motioned to one of the tall bar chairs next to the table. "Have a seat."

# CHAPTER TEN

LUCAS PULLED UP a chair to Emily and Meghan's table. Both women stared at him in a way that made him wonder if he had something stuck between his teeth or had developed a huge zit on the end of his nose.

First running his hand across his face, just in case, he motioned to the bartender and ordered a cold one.

When he turned back, both women were still staring.

"Am I missing something?"

"What makes you ask that?" Emily asked, taking a drink from the glass she held.

"You two are making me nervous."

"Who—us?" Meghan hooked her arm with Emily's, then laughed. "Then again, we get that a lot." She winked at Emily. "That we make men nervous."

Emily snorted. "Yep. All the time. Every time we come here, in fact."

He took in the two friends. Meghan was a pretty woman, but Emily was beautiful. So much so that just looking at her made his heart hiccup.

"Two beautiful women, I'd say you do make men nervous," he agreed.

"But not you?" Emily asked, watching him over the rim of her glass.

She made him nervous as hell. He knew the devastation

this woman could cause in his life. The devastation of wanting so desperately to make her happy and not being able to.

"Should I be nervous?"

"Definitely." This came from Meghan. "And so should that delicious guy who keeps smiling at me from the bar. You two have fun. I'm going to go see how nervous I can make him by asking him to buy me a drink."

Emily and Lucas watched Meghan sidle up to the bar and indeed ask the guy who'd been staring at their table to buy her a drink.

"He looks happy to oblige."

The guy did, ecstatic even.

"Do you want something else to drink?" Lucas offered.

"No. I'm good. Haven't finished this one yet." She held up her glass that was about a third full still. "I imagine I always will be a lightweight, so much so that this is soda."

He'd figured that.

"You still go out and party with the crew every chance you get?"

He thought about her question. He did go out on occasion to hang with his friends. Those times were further and further apart and not at all since he'd joined the staff at Children's. Not that the gang didn't still get together routinely, but that he just had other things he preferred doing.

"I still see them," he admitted, not bothering to explain further.

"I imagined so."

Something in her tone had him studying her a little closer. "Did you not like my friends, Emily?"

Her cheeks pinkened. "I never said that."

She didn't have to. The truth was written all over her lovely face. "You rarely wanted to go with me. It never occurred to me that it was because you didn't like my friends."

"Drinking and partying was never my thing."

True. She hadn't ever seemed to enjoy attending parties or hanging with his friends. He'd hoped she'd eventually relax around them. She never had.

"What was your thing?"

She hesitated a moment, then whispered so low he read her lips more than heard her. "You."

Her answer humbled him. He'd been such a fool. How could he have had her in his life, had her love and affection, and lost it? Of all the things he'd ever failed at, losing Emily topped the list.

He shouldn't have married her to begin with, and he sure shouldn't have divorced her once he had.

"I made a lot of mistakes, didn't I?"

Glancing away, she shrugged. "We both did."

"I didn't appreciate what I had, Emily."

She stared into her almost empty glass, then took one last sip. "Most people don't until they lose something."

"True." He didn't know what to say. He hadn't appreciated it that he'd gotten to wake up next to her each morning, that he'd gotten to go to sleep next to her at night. That at any point in between he could call her and hear her lovely voice tell him she loved him.

"Let's dance," she suggested, placing her now empty glass on the tabletop.

"Okay." Any excuse to have her in his arms would do.

He held her close, loving the way she fit next to his body, loving the way when he breathed in her sweet vanilla scent filled his nostrils.

They danced the slow song, then several upbeat ones that put a sexy sheen to Emily's skin. One that he wished he'd caused from other movements of their bodies together.

"Hey, guys, I'm outta here." Meghan interrupted their dancing. "I've got to be at work bright and early in the morning."

Emily hugged her friend goodbye. "You want me to walk with you to your apartment?"

Meghan shook her head. "I'm fine. You stay and have fun."

"What about you?" Lucas asked. "You want to stay here for a while or are you ready to go to your apartment?"

"I'm not on schedule tomorrow."

"Does that mean you want to stay?"

She met his gaze, her lips slightly parted. "What do you want, Lucas?"

For her to say his name until they were both satiated. To hold her in his arms and wake up beside her and do it all over again. Day after day. Night after night.

Where the thought came from, Lucas didn't question. Just that his whole mind filled with the overpowering response.

"Whatever you want is fine, Emily. Just so long as I get to be with you."

Emily frowned at Lucas's answer. Why, she wasn't sure. Just that it was sweet and she didn't want sweet from him.

She wanted to keep him neatly compartmentalized.

"Let's go back to my apartment."

"If that's what you want."

"That would be why I suggested it," she snapped, then instantly felt bad. He hadn't done anything wrong. She knew that. "Sorry."

"Are you okay, Emily?"

"Fine." But she was lying. To herself. To Meghan. To him. She might want to stay in control of her feelings for Lucas, but to think that was what she was doing was just downright hilarious.

She laughed. Then again.

"How many of those did you have?"

Not realizing what he meant at first, she thought of the empty soda glass she'd left on the table. "One."

"Lightweight," he accused, one corner of his mouth tugging upward.

"I'm not drunk. I told you, it was soda."

"I'm glad."

"Why?"

"Because I wouldn't have sex with a drunk woman."

"Not ever?"

"Never. Where's the pleasure in that?"

"Is that what sex is about to you?" she asked. "Pleasure?"

"Pleasure plays a big role," he admitted, his fingers tracing over her lower back. "What's sex about to you, Emily?"

"Pleasure. Nothing more," she immediately answered, refusing to give the question more thought. "Just pleasure."

Which she was feeling with her body pressed up against his. When was the music going to change back to something upbeat?

"Yet you were having sex with a man who didn't give you physical pleasure," he pointed out.

Her feet stilled. "I never said Richard didn't give me physical pleasure."

Nor did she recall telling him she'd been having sex with Richard, although maybe she had.

"Did he?"

She frowned. "You don't hear me asking about the women you've been with since our divorce, do you? You have no right to ask me about Richard or any other man."

"Have there been others, Emily?" he asked, whether he had the right or not. His body had stiffened against hers, as if he were bracing himself for her answer.

She was tempted to lie, to say that there had been dozens, many men who shamed him as a lover. But she'd never been much on untruths.

"No." She didn't elaborate.

"I'm glad."

Frustration ran up and down her spine. She pulled back to glare at him. "Really? You're glad that in the past five years I've had one lover besides you? How absolutely selfish is that when I've no doubt you've had dozens of women."

"There haven't been dozens of women, Emily." He closed his eyes, took a deep breath. "I'll be the first to admit I have no right to feel jealous of any man touching you—I gave up that right—but, Emily, I do. The thought of you being with anyone other than me rips me up inside."

"Don't say that."

"Why not?"

"Because we both know that whatever this is between us right now, it's temporary, and I don't intend to spend my life alone. There will be other men, Lucas. Someday. Maybe I'll get lucky and meet someone who can give me all the things I want first thing after you, but, if not, then I'm okay with having a few hot affairs first."

"No."

"No?"

He let out an exasperated breath. "What is it you want from a man, Emily?"

"From you or from some other man?"

"Both."

"From you, sex."

He nodded as if he knew that was going to be her answer.

"From other men?" She shrugged. "Someday, I want to meet a man whom I can have a good life with, a couple of kids, go to parent-teacher meetings and soccer games, that kind of thing."

Kids. Her heart squeezed. Would she ever have children? Did she even want to risk pregnancy again? What if she couldn't carry a pregnancy to full-term?

"You deserve that."

Oh, Lucas. If only…

"I know. I do," she agreed, wondering if there was ever a way to repair the hurt once so much had piled up on a person.

"But not with me?"

Her breath caught. "What are you saying, Lucas? You don't want those things. You don't even want kids."

He frowned. "I never said I didn't want kids."

"Sure you did," she reminded him, her fingertips curling into her palms. "When I mentioned having a baby, you shut me down real fast."

"We'd only been married a few months, Emily. You were just starting your nursing career. I was finishing up my fellowship. We were still figuring out married life. You were unhappy and I was stressed. The last thing we needed was a baby."

"Then I guess it's a good thing we didn't have one." She pulled away, unable to stand being in his arms another minute, unable to suppress the memories she never let rise to the surface. Memories she'd done her best to forget altogether.

Blindly, she made her way through the crowd on the dance floor toward the exit. She needed air.

When she stepped outside the club, she gulped in big breaths of air laced with the smell of hot dogs, pretzels and whatever else the street vendors had going.

Her heart pounded in her chest and her lungs couldn't get enough air. Why hadn't she just not answered his text? That would have been for the best. Instead, they'd gone down a conversation path she'd never wanted to take.

"Emily?"

Why had he followed her? She'd known he'd follow her. Of course he would. He'd come to the club because she was there.

She didn't open her eyes.

"Emily?"

"Go away, Lucas."

"No."

She opened her eyes. "You told me you'd leave if I asked you to."

"That was before."

"Before?"

He paused, seeming to search for the right words. "What happened back there?"

"What do you mean?"

"Your skin went green, and if I didn't know better, I'd have thought you were going to be ill. You told me you didn't have anything but soda. That shouldn't have made you sick. So tell me, what happened in there?"

"There are some things we just shouldn't talk about."

"So you were okay talking about our past lovers but not your perception that I didn't want children? Your false perception, I might add."

"No, I wasn't okay with talking about our past lovers or my perceptions. I'm not okay with any of this."

She pulled away and started walking down the street in the direction of her apartment. Her building wasn't far.

"I don't want to fight with you, Emily. I never wanted to fight with you," Lucas said from beside her just outside her apartment door.

"Odd, that's what we seem to do best."

"That's not what we do best."

"Then too bad we can't just stay naked all the time, eh?"

"Well, it's a safe bet to say you'd win every argument if that were the case."

She shook her head. "Don't make light of this, Lucas."

He touched her face, running his fingers along the edge of her hair, then cupping her nape. "I'm sorry, Emily. For whatever it was I said wrong inside the club, I am sorry.

For every mistake I ever made where you are concerned, I'm sorry. Forgive me."

She wasn't sure she could if she wanted to, but that didn't stop her body from melting against his when he pulled her inside her apartment and kissed her.

# CHAPTER ELEVEN

CASSIE BELLOWS REGAINED consciousness at some point during the night.

Apparently, Cassie's nurse had called Lucas, because he was there and in Cassie's room when Emily arrived at the hospital and took report from the night nurse.

"He's in with her right now. Has been for a while. He's such a great doctor. He's going to be a great father someday."

Emily's heart squeezed so tight in her chest that she thought she might pass out. She didn't respond to the nurse's comment. There was no need. Amy was still going on and on about Dr. Cain's many fabulous features.

"I bet you were ecstatic when he bought your TBI basket."

"Ecstatic," she agreed to keep Amy from digging deeper if she told the truth about how she'd felt about Lucas buying her basket. She liked Amy but wasn't close enough to the woman to be sharing intimate details of her life. She still felt a little nervous that she'd told Meghan about who Lucas was. She didn't want her friend's pity should things go wrong.

"How a good-looking guy like him hasn't been snapped up by some smart woman is beyond me."

"Looks aren't everything," she mumbled under her breath, not really meaning for Amy to catch her words.

"Yeah, but that man is the total package. Looks, intelligence, sense of humor, compassion and money. A girl could do a lot worse."

Ugh. How did she end up in this conversation?

"I suppose."

"Hey, all I'm saying is that if it were me he'd paid that much money to go to dinner with, I'd make sure he got his money's worth." Amy waggled her brows suggestively. "You should at least think about it. I heard you and the pharmacist broke up."

Gossip sure spread fast.

"We've already gone on our dinner date."

"And I definitely got my money's worth."

She hated how Lucas did that, walked up behind her and joined into conversations she was having. But she supposed if she was going to talk about him, he had a right to join in. Not that she'd wanted to talk about him, but it seemed she couldn't escape doing so.

Amy blushed at being caught. "Hi, Dr. Cain. We were just talking about you."

"I heard." His smile reached his eyes. "All good things, I hope?"

"Absolutely." Amy laughed a little flirtatiously. "Is there anything else to be said?"

His gaze met Emily's, as if challenging her to speak up. She kept her mouth closed.

She might have lots of negative things to say, but since she'd been having mind-blowing sex with the man, she really didn't think she had the right to point out any flaws.

"Did Amy tell you the good news?" His gaze searched Emily's. "Cassie woke up during the night."

"She mentioned that. She also mentioned you came to the hospital after she woke up and that you've been with her since."

As in, she knew he'd come here when he'd left her place, and when had he slept? Because, as handsome as he was, Emily noted the fatigue around his eyes and it pulled at her heart.

"She's going to be fine from the bleed." He sounded genuinely happy about the news. "No lasting damage that I can tell from the increased intracranial pressure."

"That's wonderful."

"I'll be taking her back to the operating room soon to remove the tumor. Just as soon as she's strong enough to withstand another surgery."

Emily nodded.

"She's going to feel like a new person when I'm finished."

"No doubt." She met his gaze. "Did you need for one of us to do something for you, Dr. Cain? Because Amy needs to finish giving me report so I can go check on my patients this morning."

It didn't surprise Emily when Lucas showed up again later that day. She was in Cassie's room and had just finished helping her mother sponge bathe the little girl. They'd just settled her back into her clean hospital bed.

"Hi, Dr. Cain," Cassie said, smiling at him despite the bandages around her head. "Are you...going...to take my blood?"

He shook his head. "You're safe from me sticking you."

"Good, because...I feel...a lot better." She truly was doing better, but one only had to listen to her speech, watch her hand and arm movements, to know that there were still serious health issues.

"I see that." He smiled back at the child. "Your color is a lot better than when I was here this morning."

"Momma says…I can…go to the playroom…soon…if I keep…getting stronger."

"Hopefully, you'll be strong enough very soon."

He ran through a check on Cassie's cranial nerves, making her smile as he asked her to make the different facial expressions at him. He puffed his cheeks out, waggled his eyebrows, smiled, frowned, furrowed his brow and gritted his teeth back at her with each check, eliciting a giggle from his patient and a smile from Cassie's mom.

He really was great with Cassie. Amy had been right. Lucas would be a great father. If only… No. Emily absolutely positively was not going to let her mind go there.

Even if her mind had been going there on and off since he'd first shown up at Children's. How could it not have?

Still, some memories were best never resurrected.

Some parts of the past she just couldn't deal with.

Not ever again.

Having lived through them the first time had almost killed her.


"Will you please go to dinner with me tonight?"

Emily bit the inside of her lip. She didn't want to date Lucas. She wanted… She wasn't sure what she wanted. Just that she was scared of going to dinner with him. She'd had fun with him at the club, dancing, but overall that experience had just left her feeling raw. Everything about being near him left her feeling vulnerable.

"I promise I won't bite."

Her gaze cut to his. "Yeah, I've heard that before."

His lips twitched. "Promises not to bite when I'm in bed don't count."

"Says who?"

"Me?"

Despite her misgivings, she laughed. "You're the final authority on biting?"

"I probably don't have near enough experience to be the final authority, but if you want to volunteer for me to practice nibbling on, I'm all for upping my game."

"I'm sure you are."

"But I'd like to take you to dinner first."

"Why?"

"I enjoy being with you and want to spend time with you."

She enjoyed being with him, too. Naked, no problem. That was easy to categorize into just sex. But spending time with Lucas with her clothes on? That wasn't so easy to justify away from work.

"I'd like to take you to this little French bistro off Broadway. They have this fresh-baked bread that just melts in your mouth."

"And straight onto my hips."

"Your hips are perfect, Emily."

His compliment came out as sincere and not one meant to puff her up. She liked that. Liked that he sounded as if he truly believed what he said.

"But they won't be if I indulge in fresh-baked bread," she pointed out, trying not to get too elated that he'd said her hips were perfect. He made her feel perfect. When he looked at her, touched her, with such awe, how could she not?

He'd always done that in the beginning, made her feel good about herself, made her feel as if she was the only woman in the world and the center of his existence.

"I promise to make you burn every single carbohydrate before the sun comes up."

She rolled her eyes. "I know what will be coming up before the sun."

He grinned. "You know me so well."

Yes, she did. And yet she didn't. Not anymore. He'd

changed in the years they'd been apart. He was more mature, more stable these days, more caring and aware of others around him. Then again, he was five years older, a man in his thirties. Of course he'd matured.

"Does that mean you'll give me the privilege of taking you to a late dinner for two?"

She sighed, then nodded. It wasn't as if she could say no. Even if she could, all she'd do was think about him and hope he showed at her apartment. What would be the point of saying no? "But only if you promise to make me enjoy every second of carb-burning."

His grin was lethal. "Was there ever any doubt?"

No, that, Emily never doubted.

Emily's menu hadn't had prices, but she didn't need dollar signs to know she was in a restaurant way out of her price ballpark. Part of her wanted to question Lucas about wasting so much money on taking her to eat at such a place when she'd have enjoyed grabbing a pretzel dog and walking around Times Square to people watch just as much.

Well, almost as much.

She had to admit the cozy candlelit booth with just the two of them was nice. Perhaps a bit too over-the-top romantic for a divorced couple. Then again, most divorced couples weren't having hot sex every night, either.

Or maybe they were. What did she know about such things other than that Lucas got to her physically as much as he ever did? The absence of the golden band he'd slipped onto her finger so long ago hadn't changed that one bit.

Not really.

"You got quiet. Should I be worried?"

"I was thinking about when you put my wedding band on my finger." Automatically, her thumb brushed across the empty spot. She'd never been much of a jewelry person, and these days she chose not to wear any rings unless it was a fun, chunky costume piece that complemented whatever she was wearing.

His expression tightened. "What about it?"

She shrugged. "Not really anything specific. I was just thinking about you doing so."

"Do you still have your rings, Emily?"

Wondering if she should admit such craziness, she nodded. "I thought about selling them, but there just seemed something weird about doing so. I guess keeping them is just as weird."

"I've still got mine, too."

"You do?" Why did that surprise her? Why did some deep part of her rejoice that he'd held on to his wedding band? It didn't mean anything that he'd kept the ring. The only thing that meant anything was the legal divorce document that had torn away any meaning the ring had once held.

He nodded. "Like you, I've thought about getting rid of it but never have."

"We were too young," she mused.

"That's what everyone said." His gaze met hers. "But the truth of the matter is that I was older than you are now."

Her eyes widened a little. "You were, weren't you?"

Not that she hadn't known, just that she hadn't thought about it. He'd seemed much younger at the time than she currently felt. Maybe because he'd still been working on his education and had still lived in his parents' home.

"I'd led a pretty sheltered life up until I got to medical school," he admitted, echoing her thoughts. "It was harder work than I'd anticipated."

"You always made excellent grades." She knew he had. She'd seen the academic awards he'd won throughout his college and pre-college years.

"That was easy. Medical school not so much so. I struggled a lot more than I let people see."

Odd, she'd never thought of him as struggling. Then again, by the time she'd met him, he'd been doing his surgical fellowship. Maybe she'd missed a lot of the struggling times.

"A lot more than I let you see," he added, squashing her theory.

"I remember you studying and looking up stuff on patients, but you seemed to blow through it with ease."

"Because I'd rather be playing with you than studying."

What he was saying sank in. "If I made your education more difficult, I apologize. I never wanted to interfere with any of your dreams."

He started to speak but didn't as their waiter showed up with some of the bread Lucas had bragged about.

"Mmm, this is worth every thigh jiggle," she admitted after the first buttered bite.

Lucas didn't say anything, and when she looked up and met his blue gaze, his eyes were dark. "You're beautiful, Emily. If I failed to tell you that back then, let me constantly remind you now. You. Are. Beautiful."

Where had that come from? She'd been blabbering on about food and jiggling thighs and he was proclaiming her beautiful? What was up with that?

"So are you." Because what else could she say? That once upon a time he'd made her feel like the most beautiful woman on the planet? That once upon a time when he'd looked at her she'd known he thought her the most beautiful thing he'd ever seen and she'd thought she'd be his forever?

That once upon a time she hadn't been able to look at him without bursting into tears because she'd been pregnant with his baby and he'd no longer wanted her or their child?

Lucas loved to watch Emily eat. Always had, but he'd forgotten. When she'd stuck the piece of bread in her mouth and licked her fingers, he'd sincerely thought about asking for a lick himself. Her eyes had filled with heaven, her face had relaxed in pleasure, and her sounds of enjoyment had only added to his longings.

But it was more than the physical.

With Emily, it always had been more.

He enjoyed her. Watching her. Listening to her. Talking to her. Touching her, and not just in a sexual way, although there was always that. Life just seemed better with Emily.

A lot better with Emily.

Then again, the problem had been her unhappiness, not his.

"You're making me nervous," she said, drawing his gaze back to hers.

He took her hand into his and brought her fingers to his lips. He pressed a kiss there. "You have no reason to ever be nervous around me, Emily."

"Right." She pulled her hand away and tucked it under her leg. "Because you're as harmless as a hungry lion."

"Perhaps, but I'd never intentionally hurt you. Despite what you may believe, I always wanted to make you happy."

But he hadn't been able to make her happy, had hurt her, and the truth of that hung in the air between them.

How had Lucas convinced Emily to go for drinks at the top of a hotel with a revolving restaurant so they could view the New York City night skyline?

It wasn't as if she hadn't lived here her whole life. She knew what the city looked like. She'd guess most everyone in the restaurant were tourists except them.

"You guys need anything?" their waitress asked. There was a one drink minimum, but they'd both ordered bottles of water rather than anything alcoholic.

Just being with Lucas made her feel drunk.

Or maybe it was the slowly turning restaurant.

But she doubted it. The room turned at a pace where you didn't realize you were even moving until you started watching the buildings around you.

"Admit it, this was a good idea."

She fought to keep her gaze from going to his no doubt smug expression. "I suppose."

"What would you have rather done?"

He sounded as if there was nothing she could say that would top what they currently did. She had to admit, the evening had been nice, talking with him had been nice even, but she wasn't admitting those things.

"Gone back to my place?" she suggested.

"My bad. You win." He stood, pulled a money clip from his front pocket and tossed a bill onto their table.

"Lucas." She laughed, tugging on his arm. "Sit down."

"But you said…" Grinning, his eyes full of mischief, he sat back down.

"We're here now. I want to see if I can see the Statue of Liberty from up here."

"I was told that you once could, but new buildings have gone up since this one was built and have blocked the view."

Disappointment filled her. "Oh."

"I'd take you there if you want to see Lady Liberty."

"I've been before." On an elementary school field trip, they'd taken the ferry out to the island and toured the statue. She'd been in total awe of the size and magnificence of such a gift symbolizing freedom. She'd often wondered if any country had given another such a glorious present.

"Sometimes things are better the second time around."

She hesitated only a moment before agreeing. "I guess we could go. It has been quite a few years since I visited."

"I've never been."

She looked at him in disbelief. "What?"

He shrugged. "It's not that big of a deal. I've just never been out on the island."

"Which means you've never gone up in the statue, either?"

"No."

"Well, that's just sad."

A wry smile played on his lips. "There goes my image of a childhood full of privilege."

"Oh, that image is still there," she didn't hesitate to point out. "Now, I just wonder how many educational gaps were there, too."

"Educational gaps?"

"Things like trips to the Statue of Liberty. Poor, poor Lucas."

"I've been to the Eiffel Tower, does that count? It's French, too."

The Eiffel Tower because he truly did come from a background of privilege. He'd once told her that the year after he'd graduated from high school he'd "backpacked" Europe with some friends, whatever that had meant.

The farthest from home she'd ever been was New Jersey.

She'd never really had a reason to leave New York. Everything she'd needed was here.

Maybe someday she'd travel and see some of the world's more exotic cities. She loved the night lights, the excitement of big cities with lots of people from every walk of life within close distance. She loved the access to so many different cultures and restaurants and shops and...

"Maybe I could take you there someday."

"To the Eiffel Tower?" Her eyes widened. "Why would you do that?"

"Don't sound so shocked, Emily. Why wouldn't I want to take you to Paris? You'd love the city, the food, the people."

Good grief. Had he been reading her mind or what?

"Paris is a long way from New York."

"Not that far."

"Just a hop, skip and jump over the ocean," she mused.

"I was serious when I offered to take you."

"Thank you, but I'll pass."

"Why?"

"Because women don't go to Paris with their ex-husbands."

"Perhaps they should."

"Why?"

"To sit by the Seine, drink a cup of coffee and watch the sun rise. To visit the Louvre and so many other fascinating places. To eat a superbly cooked meal with a view of the Eiffel Tower while the sun sets."

"As if I'd want to get out of bed that early in the morning while on vacation." Anything to throw her focus anywhere but on what he was saying because he made her want to do all the things he said. With him. The harsh reality was that, despite their little sexual interlude, if she ever did see Paris, it wouldn't be with Lucas. And now if she ever did, she'd be battling the images he'd just put in her mind.

She bit the inside of her lip.

"Yet again, you do make a valid point," he agreed. "Perhaps we'd skip the early-morning sitting by the Seine and just watch the sun come up from our hotel-room bed."

She took a drink from her water.

"I should have brought you to Paris for our honeymoon."

"I couldn't have enjoyed our honeymoon any more if you'd brought me to Paris, or London, or any other exotic locale you can think of."

"Because Atlantic City is the most romantic city in the world?" he teased.

"That weekend, it was perfect," she answered in all honesty.

His gaze searched hers, but for what she wasn't sure. She

didn't say anything and for the longest time neither did he. When he did, his words were poignant.

"I believe you may be right about that, Emily. That weekend was the best of my life."

"Cheap hotel, cheap food, playing on a crowded public New Jersey boardwalk and beach… I doubt that, but we did have a good time."

His brows veed. "Why you can't believe me, I don't understand, but, yes, we did have a good time."

Memories of that weekend shook her, and when she looked at him, she knew he was flooded with similar ones. Did he also wonder how something that had been so perfect had gone so wrong?

"I'd like to take you back to your place and make love to you now, Emily Stewart."

She wasn't going to argue. She wanted that, too.

Perhaps, if she was honest, she'd admit she'd never stopped wanting him to do that.

Then his words hit her. He hadn't said he wanted to go have sex with her.

He'd said he wanted to make love to her.

No. She shouldn't read anything into his words. That was all they'd been. Words.

They'd be having sex. Not making love.

At least, Lucas would.

More and more, Emily questioned exactly what it was she was doing with Lucas.

# CHAPTER TWELVE

WHEN THEY GOT to her apartment, Lucas undressed her slowly, kissing and caressing each newly uncovered area of her body.

By the time she stood in only her panties, she ached for him, but he wasn't finished with his sweet torture.

"How come I'm the only one with my clothes off?" she demanded, tugging at his shirt.

"Because you're the one who's exquisite."

"You're good with the lines, Lucas. Keep them coming and you're liable to get lucky."

"I'm definitely getting lucky. Actually, I already have. I'm here with you."

"See, that's what I mean with the lines. Good job," she praised as she undid his shirt buttons and pushed the material aside to reveal his chest. She groaned at the masterpiece she unveiled. "It should be illegal to cover that up."

He laughed. "Good thing it's not. I'd freeze during winter."

"A frozen Lucas. I'd have a lick of that."

"I'd let you and imagine I'd thaw pretty fast with your hot mouth anywhere near me."

She bent, kissed his belly, felt him suck in his breath, saw the goosebumps that covered his skin. She'd done that. Her touch. Her kiss. Sure, maybe he reacted to lots of women, but right now, at this moment, he was with her and it was her touch he craved.

She craved to touch. To kiss. To lick. To taste every inch of him.

So she did.

When neither of them could stand more, he positioned himself above her, paused, stared at her with so much emotion in his eyes that she felt overwhelmed. What was he waiting for?

"I've missed you, Emily. So much." Rather than giving her what she ached for, he kissed her mouth. A kiss way too sweet for the heat of the moment.

A kiss way too sweet for her peace of mind.

His gaze locked with hers, he moved his hips, giving her what she needed, what they needed.

Rather than the frenzy of their previous matings, he kept his pace slow. When she'd try to increase it, he'd resist. When she gripped his buttocks, urging him faster, deeper, he took her hands into his and held them above her head, locking them into place by his hand over her wrists. She didn't really try to escape. Why should she when the heat was rising inside her thighs, when warmth swirled in her belly, building?

His gaze still locked with hers, he built her higher until she went so high there was nowhere to go but over the edge.

So she fell.

Further and further, she floated downward.

He let her float, but not all the way down. Instead, he moved and took her up, up, up again.

And again.

Chest heaving, Lucas collapsed onto the mattress next to Emily. Her chest rose and fell. Her lips were swollen from his kisses. Her body flushed from his loving. Her hair fanned out around her in messy, just-had-wild-sex disarray.

He'd never seen anything more erotic. He'd never seen anything more beautiful.

"You need to get dressed," she told him, her voice breathy. "So you can go home before it gets any later. I have to work tomorrow."

Then there was that.

"I don't want to go, Emily."

"I don't want you to stay."

Which was a hard pill to swallow.

"Why not?"

"We aren't dating, Lucas. We aren't moving toward a relationship with each other. We're using each other for sex. Nothing more. For you to stay in my bed, to actually sleep beside me, implies an intimacy we don't have."

"What if I want that intimacy with you?"

"This isn't just about what you want."

"I realize that, but—"

"No buts, Lucas." She climbed out of the bed and grabbed his underwear off the floor and tossed it at him. "Here."

"What are you afraid of, Emily?"

Rather than climb back into bed, she opened a dresser drawer and pulled out an oversize New York Knicks T-shirt and put it on. "With you? Everything."

That had him pausing with his boxer briefs halfway up his thighs. "After what we just shared, how could you possibly be afraid of me?"

"That was sex."

He shook his head. "You keep telling yourself that, Emily, but we both know that wasn't just sex. Never was. Never will be."

Panic filled her eyes. "That's all it can be."

"Why? I want a relationship with you, Emily. I want to be the man in your life. The man you fall asleep next to and wake up beside."

The thought of her sinking back into depression, of him stealing her happiness, terrified him, but maybe they could have a relationship that built upon the good between them.

She stood beside the bed watching him, but she looked ready to run if he so much as moved toward her. "I won't ever marry you again."

"Nor would I ask you to. Marriage is where we messed up."

"Marriage is where we messed up?" She shook her head as if trying to process what he meant. "How did marriage mess anything up?"

"You were so sad after we got married, Emily." He didn't know how else to answer her question, but obviously marriage had ruined their relationship.

"We are what messed up our relationship, Lucas. Me and you. We would have fallen apart whether we had been married or not. We may have phenomenal sex, but we were never destined to be together."

"You're wrong."

"You think we were destined to be together?" she scoffed.

Did he?

"I think there's something between you and me that we don't share with anyone else."

"It's called sexual chemistry."

"It's more than sex."

She rolled her eyes. "How's this for irony? The woman is trying to keep sex as just sex and the guy is trying to attach feelings to the physical."

He shrugged. "The truth doesn't change regardless of how we label it."

"The truth? The truth is that you shouldn't be here, that we are divorced and should start acting like it."

What she was saying sank in.

"You don't want to see me anymore?"

"I never wanted to see you to begin with, Lucas. I was fine, just fine, until you came back into my life with all your potent sex appeal and fancy orgasms."

That had him stopping, grinning a little despite their conversation. "I gave you fancy orgasms?"

She threw her hands into the air.

"Sorry, but a man likes to hear that he gave his woman orgasms, and when she calls them fancy, he definitely wants to hear more."

Her hands went to her hips. "I'm not your woman."

There was that.

"You used to be."

"In the past. Doesn't matter anymore. The past is gone."

"The past is never really gone. It's the culmination of all the past that makes up the present."

That one earned him another eye roll. "Oh, don't go spouting your Harvard Philosophy 101 at me."

"Are you purposely trying to fight with me, Emily? Because I refuse to fight with you. If you want me to go, I'll go. But not without you knowing that it's not because I want to go. What I want is to be with you and to sleep with you in my arms."

She sank onto the edge of the bed and stared at him. "You're crazy."

Yeah, he was.

"About you." With that, he leaned over and kissed her forehead. "Good night, Emily. Sweet dreams."

A couple of weeks later, Emily was on duty when Kevin Rogers was admitted. He was a four-year-old pedestrian who'd been a hit-and-run victim. According to eyewitnesses, a taxi driver had driven up on a sidewalk while glancing down at his cell phone, hit the boy, then disappeared quickly.

The boy had been admitted with multiple fractures and

traumatic brain injury. The emergency-room physician had given him poor odds of surviving.

The CT of his head had shown active brain bleeds. If he wasn't taken to surgery to relieve the pressure and stop the bleeds, he'd be dead before midnight. If he did manage to survive, he'd likely have permanent damage from the increased pressure on delicate brain tissue.

Probably because Emily had volunteered when Cassie Bellows had needed emergency surgery, Emily's charge nurse had informed her she was being shifted over to the operating room to assist Dr. Cain along with the rest of the assembled surgical team.

"But I have patients," she reminded her, not wanting to go back into the operating room with Lucas.

"Meghan and Amy are down to one patient. I was going to have to send one of them home. I'm going to reassign Jenny and Cassie to them and send you to the OR rather than someone having to be called in."

What the nurse manager said made perfect sense. But Emily fought the urge to beg the woman not to make her.

Although she opened her apartment door to Lucas night after night, she tried to avoid him as much as possible at the hospital. She didn't want others to see how he affected her. She didn't want others to associate them together.

She didn't want to deal with the aftermath at work when things fell apart.

Been there, done that, had ended up leaving the job.

Whereas during Cassie's surgery Emily had been assigned care of Cassie, this time she was assigned to directly assist Lucas.

Which meant she'd be right beside him.

Which meant there was no avoiding him.

Which meant she'd have to touch him, albeit through sterile gloves and under harsh lights and circumstances.

She was still mentally bemoaning having to assist Lucas

while she scrubbed up. It wasn't that she didn't enjoy being in the surgical suite. She'd enjoyed the time she'd worked there, but she'd missed direct patient care.

She entered the surgical suite, made sure she had everything Lucas would need on her tray and winced a little on the inside at how tiny the boy looked on the hospital bed when he was wheeled in.

A sterile decked-out Lucas followed him into the suite and the surgical team jumped in to try to save the little boy.

An hour into the procedure, Emily was dabbing sweat from Lucas's forehead and studying the exhaustion showing on his face.

An hour later, he still meticulously worked, doing all he could to stop the tiny bleeds in the boy's brain.

By the time Lucas finished, Emily's heart hurt for him, but because of the others in the room, she didn't say anything, didn't offer comfort.

The surgery had gone past the end of her shift, so she performed the rest of her duties, cleaning her area, changing back into her own scrubs from the hospital-issue surgical scrubs, then clocked out.

Prior to heading home, she went by to check on Jenny and Cassie and was pleased to find them stable.

She swung by a take-out shop and picked up enough food for two. Who knew if Lucas would have eaten when he came by later that night?

Only, as the clock minutes ticked by, Lucas still hadn't shown at close to 1:00 a.m. Unable to stand it anymore, worried about where he was, but not wanting to wake him if he had just gone home to sleep, she texted him.

Where are you?

Within seconds her phone sounded with a texted reply and relief spread through her body.

Outside your door.

*What?* She got out of bed and practically ran to her living-room door, peeped through the viewer and undid the chain and dead bolt.

"Why didn't you knock?"

"I left the hospital and had just gotten off the elevator when your text came through."

"Oh."

"Did you miss me?"

She could lie. She could tell him she hadn't. But he looked so exhausted, so much as if he needed her to tell the truth, that she did.

"Yes."

"Good." That was all he said. Good. Then he stepped inside her apartment, waited while she relocked the door and safety chain, then took her in his arms.

"What took you so long?"

"Kevin Rogers died."

Emily's breath caught. The little boy had died?

"Oh, Lucas!" She winced, then wrapped her arms around him. "I'm sorry. You did all you could."

"Did I?"

His question caught her off guard. "Of course you did. I was next to you all those hours you searched for bleeds, making sure you stopped each one."

"Obviously, it wasn't enough."

She hugged him. "You aren't God, Lucas. You can't heal what's too broken to mend."

"I know that, but that little boy shouldn't have died. He was too young to die."

"Age has nothing to do with injuries. You know that."

He swiped his hands through his hair. "Is it okay if I take a quick shower? I headed straight here and I'm a mess."

She nodded. "Have you eaten?"

He shook his head.

"Lucas, you've got to take better care of yourself. You don't sleep. You don't eat. What am I going to do with you?"

"Let me shower, then I'll show you exactly what you can do with me."

"I'm going to heat you up something to eat while you shower. After you've eaten, we can discuss whatever you want to show me."

"Deal."

The shower had turned off long ago, but Lucas still hadn't joined her in the kitchen, where she'd heated up the leftover takeout she'd brought home.

She'd put on hot tea and sipped on a cup while she waited.

Bless him that he'd taken the boy's death so hard. That, she understood. Didn't she feel a similar responsibility for each person she took care of?

She'd had patients die over the years. When you took care of the seriously ill, death happened.

No doubt Lucas had lost patients in the past, too, but something about Kevin Rogers had clearly gotten to him.

She glanced at her cellular phone, noting the time. He'd been in her bathroom for a long time. Was he okay?

Intent on knocking on the bathroom door to see if he needed anything, she went to her bedroom and stopped just inside the room. Lucas lay on her bed, his hair damp, nothing on but a towel about his waist, and he was out cold.

"Lucas?"

No change in the even rise and fall of his chest.

"Lucas?" She had to wake him. He couldn't stay.

Only, he still didn't stir. Could she really wake him and send him away when he was so completely exhausted?

She winced.

She didn't want him to sleep in her bed.

But she couldn't bring herself to wake him.

She walked back into the kitchen, put away the food, flipped off the lights, stared at her sofa for long minutes contemplating how comfortable it would be, then sighed.

She didn't have to work tomorrow, but she didn't think she'd sleep a wink on the sofa, either.

Lucas wasn't the only one exhausted.

With her heart pounding and her insides shaking, she went back into the bedroom, studied the sleeping man in her bed.

A man she'd loved. A man she'd hated.

A man… What was it she felt for him now?

She didn't love him. She didn't hate him.

What was this feeling inside her? Definitely, she felt something. Sexual chemistry as she'd claimed? Yes, she felt that, but there was more.

Looking closer, she noted the redness around his eyes.

Dear Lord. He looked as if he'd been crying.

Emily swallowed the knot that formed.

Had he cried in the shower over Kevin Rogers's death?

Her heart tightened to where she couldn't breathe.

Forget the sofa. She crossed the room, turned off the lamplight and snuggled up against a man she suddenly wanted to comfort and protect from the whole world.

Not a feeling she welcomed. Not a feeling she wanted.

But she hugged him and fell asleep with her arm wrapped around him all the same.

# CHAPTER THIRTEEN

LUCAS WOKE JUST as light began streaking into the room. A room he'd never seen bathed in the colors of sunrise.

Emily's bedroom.

She'd let him stay the night after they'd had sex.

He frowned. Actually, she'd let him stay even though they hadn't had sex. Emotionally and physically exhausted from Kevin's surgery, then death, he'd lain down meaning to catch only a few minutes of shut-eye to get a second wind and he'd passed out.

Occasionally, a patient got beneath his skin and just got to him. The boy and the utter loss in his parents' eyes when he'd met with them had done so. He'd wanted to be the hero, to repair what he'd known going in might not be fixable. He'd failed and that hadn't been an easy pill to swallow.

Why hadn't Emily awakened him and sent him home?

It was what he'd have expected. Only, she hadn't. She'd crawled into the bed next to him and at some point they'd gotten under the covers. Currently, her backside was spooned up against him and he held her close.

He took a deep breath, catching a faint whiff of vanilla.

Emily.

His Emily.

He kissed the top of her head and realized there was no-where in the world he'd rather be than holding her.

His ex-wife.

Closing his eyes, he buried his face in her hair and held her close. He wasn't scheduled with patients today, wasn't on call at the hospital. Emily had worked the past three days. She should be off today, too.

If she'd let him, he'd spend the day with her doing whatever she wanted to do.

Until then, he'd count his blessings.

Even on her days off work, Emily tended to wake bright and early. This morning had been different. She'd been snuggled against a hard male body and she'd slept hours later than she usually did.

Then again, so had Lucas.

She twisted around to look at him. His eyes were closed, but she wasn't sure if he was asleep or awake.

"Good morning, Emily."

Awake. Heat infused her face. "Morning."

His eyes opened and he smiled and whatever embarrassment she'd been feeling at getting caught looking at him disappeared.

"Sorry I passed out on you last night."

"I guess you were tired."

"I guess I was. Thank you for not throwing me out."

"We both know it was probably a mistake in letting you stay."

"How do you figure?"

"Sleeping together is too intimate."

"Sex isn't?"

"Sex is…sex."

"Make no mistake, there is shared intimacy when having sex, Emily."

"I know that. You're not understanding what I mean."

"Actually, I probably do. You want to keep distinct boundaries that everything between us is only physical."

"Exactly," she agreed, smiling, glad he understood.

"It's not going to work."

Her smile faded. "Why not?"

"Because I want more than physical with you."

She scooted away from him, sat up and pulled her knees to her. "I can't be friends with you, Lucas. I just can't."

"Why not?"

"Too much has happened between us for you and me to be friends."

"We can be lovers, but not friends?"

"I get the feeling you're laughing at me. Whether you understand or not, I'm serious."

"I know you are and I don't mean to tease you, Emily."

"Sure you don't."

"Okay, so maybe I do a little. I always enjoyed teasing you. Like the time I…" He launched into a story about when she'd met his best friend.

"How is Hank?"

"Still same old Hank."

"Does he know you're working with me?"

Lucas nodded. "He knows."

"And?"

"And nothing."

"He didn't warn you that you were crazy or question why you were taking a job that would force you to see your ex-wife day after day?"

"No, he didn't."

"Why is that?"

"Good question, and one you'd have to ask him."

"I doubt I'll ever see him again."

"We could go out with him and his wife tonight."

"Hank is married?"

"Two years ago. His wife just found out she's pregnant a few months ago."

Pregnant. Emily's empty uterus spasmed. Lucas almost

sounded envious, but she knew better. Or maybe she didn't. He'd said she'd been wrong about his not wanting children.

Was that what had driven him to seek her out? That his best friend had settled down and Lucas realized he was the odd man out?

The possibility seemed hard to fathom, but just his being there, having taken a job at Children's, telling her he wanted to have a relationship with her, his ex-wife, all of it was hard to take in.

"Do you think we'd have kids by now if we hadn't divorced?"

Lucas's question gutted her as surely as if he'd stabbed her. She leaped out of the bed. "It's too early in the morning for questions like those."

Not glancing his way, she rushed into the bathroom, shut and locked the door. She slid down to the floor and cried tears she refused to let have sound no matter how badly her body shook.

From the time Emily had emerged from the bathroom, Lucas knew something was different.

There was a hollowness to her eyes, a blankness to her facial expression that told a deeper story.

Plus, she hadn't met his eyes a single time. Not even when he'd cupped her chin and tried to get her to.

She was shutting him out and he felt the gap between them widening with every breath she took.

She was going to end things. In his gut, he knew she was.

A desperation hit him.

He didn't want Emily ending things between them.

He needed her.

A heavy realization to make.

He needed his ex-wife.

"I'm going to call the hospital and find out what Kevin Rogers's funeral arrangements are. I feel I should go."

Staring into her cup of coffee, Emily nodded.

"Will you go with me, Emily?"

She glanced up, looking like a deer caught in the head-lights. "Why?" Her voice squeaked.

"I'm not good at funerals, and especially not a kid's."

"I—" Her expression pinched. "Lucas, we really don't need to be spending so much time together."

He'd known it was coming, but her words still punched at him.

"Please go with me."

Her inner turmoil was palpable in the room, but in the end she nodded. "If you want me there."

"I want you there." He needed her there, at his side, where she belonged.

Because Emily belonged beside him.

And he belonged beside her.

The tortured scowl on her face said now wasn't the time to go spouting off about past feelings he'd realized weren't in the past, but present at this very moment.

"What would you like to do today, Emily? I'd really like to spend the day with you."

Did Lucas not hear anything she said? Hadn't Emily just said they didn't need to be spending so much time together?

Yet she'd agreed to go to a funeral with him. Because the memory of how he'd looked when he'd shown up at her apartment, at how his red puffy eyes had looked even in sleep, had left her unable to do anything other than be there.

She hated that.

She hated how entangled he was becoming in her life. If she didn't put a stop to it, every aspect of her life would soon be taken over by him. Then what?

She knew.

If she let Lucas invade everything, when he moved on

to the next phase of his life, she'd be a devastated wreck as she'd been five years ago.

Only, she wouldn't. Not this time.

She was stronger. She'd picked herself up, rebuilt a life for herself even after suffering horrendous blows. She was a survivor, and no matter what he did, she would survive. Plus, she didn't have crazy hormones influencing how she thought, causing a constant flow of tears.

But she wasn't so masochistic as to continue to let him worm his way into her very being.

She needed time away from him.

"I have other plans today, Lucas." Actually, she really did. She was taking a bus to Brooklyn to visit her parents.

Then again, her mother might take one look at her and know Lucas was back. That wouldn't go over well. Maybe she'd bail on her parents and spend the day running errands or something.

"Can't you change them?"

She shook her head. "I can't."

"I'd hoped to take you to visit the Statue of Liberty."

"Tempting, but no, thanks. I'm going to my parents'."

He winced. "I guess I wouldn't be a welcomed addition."

"Not if I want to keep my father out of jail."

"That bad?"

Her parents had never thought she should marry Lucas, didn't believe in divorce, but had comforted her after the demise of her marriage and the aftermath. Lucas showing up on their doorstep would be that bad.

"You divorced his baby girl, what do you think?"

Despite fear her mother would see right through her, Emily opted to still go see her parents. Her mother eyed her suspiciously, but, other than to ask her if she'd changed her hair, she hadn't pried.

Emily hadn't stayed long for fear she might break down

and spill everything. Her mother had been there during that awful time after she'd left Lucas. Her poor mama didn't deserve to have those worries put on her, so Emily kept silent, hugged them bye and headed out.

That was when she caught sight of the majestic lady standing tall in the Hudson Bay.

Without really questioning herself, she bought a ticket and rode the ferry out to the island, poked around, read facts and wished she'd been able to reserve in time to go to the top.

"Emily?"

She spun, surprised to see the man she'd said goodbye to that morning standing near the base of the statue. "What are you doing here?"

"I mentioned bringing you here this morning, remember?"

Yes, she remembered. "I said no, thanks."

"Yet we're both here." He gave a whimsical look, as if he couldn't believe she was there. "I decided to go for a walk to clear my head. I ended up buying a ticket, riding in the top of one of those tour-bus things and taking a ferry here."

"You rode on top of one of those tour buses?" She couldn't picture him having done so.

"Yep." He reached in his pocket and pulled out a receipt. "I even have proof."

"Why?"

"Someone accused me of having educational gaps. I filled in quite a few as the tour guide informed me where all the celebs live in Manhattan."

"I'm not sure riding in one of those tour buses counts as filling in educational gaps."

"Believe me, gaps were filled during that experience."

She narrowed her gaze. He was smiling, looked more relaxed and rested than she'd seen him look in days.

"Maybe I need to take a ride, too."

"I'd buy you a ticket."

"I can buy my own ticket," she immediately said.

"I know, but sometimes I'd like to buy you things, Emily, and surely a bus ticket isn't something you'd find offensive."

"Fine." She pressed her lips tightly together and smiled. "Let's go ride on top of a bus."

The ferry ride back to Battery Park was uneventful. They stood outside and the mist of the bay probably kinked Emily's hair, but she didn't care.

When they arrived, Lucas bought her a bus tour ticket, and they took seats at the back. It wasn't crowded, so it was only the two of them on the back row of five seats. They took the middle ones and Lucas immediately took her hand into his.

Emily was tempted to pull away but didn't want him to question why she did so when it was just holding hands and they'd done so much more over the past few weeks.

Yet his big strong hand laced with hers seemed to signify so much that wasn't real. Would never be real.

The more she didn't acknowledge that, didn't deal with that, the harder all this became.

A half hour later, Lucas squeezed her hand and grinned. "Admit it. This is fun."

"Exhilarating," she said halfheartedly. Actually, she was enjoying the tour but kept battling that she'd ended up spending the day with him anyway.

He laughed. "Tell me what you really think."

She rolled her eyes. "Fine, the weather is great."

It was. Not too cool. Not too hot.

"The company is great, too."

"And so modest."

"I meant that you were great company, Emily. Not me."

"You're not so bad."

"But you don't really want to be with me."

No, she didn't. Yet she did.

"You have to admit, our being together is pretty crazy."

"Crazier things have happened than you and me getting back together."

Back together? Where had that come from?

"We're not back together, Lucas."

"Maybe we should."

She shook her head. "No, we shouldn't."

"Why not?"

"Because…" She struggled to come up with a verbal answer, but a thousand reasons floated just beyond her tongue's reach. She knew they did.

"It's not something we have to decide at this moment, Emily. But I've told you a dozen times how much I want you in my life. You need to think about what you want."

"I can't do this, Lucas. I thought I could, but I can't."

Had she really just said that while on top of a tour bus with a bunch of tourists? Sure, the closest ones were a few seats up, but this wasn't a place for a private conversation.

Concern darkened his face. "You're getting motion sick?"

"Us, not the tour bus." Although, suddenly she couldn't do that anymore, either. Fortunately, the bus pulled over to a stop. Emily stood and headed to the front of the bus and the stairs that would lead her out of it.

She took off walking down the street, glad they were in a part of the city she recognized and that wasn't too many blocks from where she lived.

"Emily, please don't leave me like that."

He'd followed her. Of course he'd followed her. Had she really thought he wouldn't? Had she even wanted him not to?

She was the problem. Her and her mixed-up emotions.

She wanted him, but she didn't want him. Hadn't her crazy emotions been a problem before, too? She'd not been able to stop the tears, to control the mood surges that had caused her to pick fights with him. Her hormones had been all over the place. She didn't want to remember, didn't want to think about the past, about her relationship with Lucas and how everything had fallen apart. About why everything had fallen apart.

Berating herself and her weakness where he was concerned, she kept walking without answering him.

He grabbed her arm, halting her. "What's wrong, Emily? Talk to me. Please talk to me."

Now fighting tears that she had no idea where they came from, she shook her head, pulled loose and resumed walking.

He stayed beside her but didn't try to stop her again.

When they reached her building, she turned to him.

"I'm sorry, Lucas. I feel I'm an emotional wreck these days and I just…I just had to get off the bus." She didn't say *and away from him*, but the words dangled between them.

He studied her. "I've done this to you, haven't I?"

She shrugged. "I'd be lying if I said I was expecting you to show back up in my life. I wasn't prepared for a second emotional roller-coaster ride with you. I don't want to do this anymore. I want my normal, calm life back."

"You were happier before I came back into your life?"

"Yeah, I was," she said and meant it. At least, she thought she did. At the moment, everything was swirling in her mind. "Continuing this only spells disaster for me and I want off the ride before we crash."

# CHAPTER FOURTEEN

LUCAS HAD CONSIDERED skipping out on Kevin Rogers's funeral but in the end had opted to attend.

Currently, he sat in a church pew, listening to the pastor doing the funeral service recite accounts of the little boy's life and how he'd been a blessing to his parents.

Surprisingly, Emily sat next to him. She wore a pretty black dress that was classy and made her eyes sparkle like emeralds.

He wasn't holding her hand and was acutely aware of that fact. For that matter, he was acutely aware of the fact that he'd not seen her or spoken to her or kissed her or made love to her for the past two days. He'd done his best to avoid her, to give her what she wanted. He'd stayed away.

She'd been waiting on the steps when he'd arrived at the church. She'd looked tense, as if she didn't want to be there.

She could have not shown. Not Emily. She was always one to fulfill her responsibilities.

Despite how uncomfortable she'd appeared, she'd also taken his breath. Lord, he missed her.

Only the memory of her depression, knowing that he'd caused her sadness, had given him the power to honor her request of staying away. Still, he'd struggled, had wanted to take her in his arms and demand she tell him what it was about him that caused her to hurt inside so much.

Was that why he'd stayed away all these years? Because

he'd watched a bubbly young woman turn into a sad, depressed shell of herself and he'd blamed himself?

He should have talked to her back then, explained how he felt, enlisted her parents' help in getting her depression treated. He'd have gone to counseling with her, would have done whatever it took.

Emily deserved a good life, a happy life. If she felt he was a complication she didn't need, that she was happier without him, he'd leave her alone.

Maybe he'd even leave Children's because having to see her would be torture knowing he could never have her.

He'd hate to leave Children's, but he wouldn't submit Emily, or himself, to having to see each other daily. Nor would he submit himself to having to see her meet and fall in love with someone else.

She wanted a husband, kids, a family.

He wanted those things, too. With Emily.

*With Emily*, the thought echoed through his mind.

He glanced over at her, thinking he'd just sneak a quick look, but frowned at what he saw.

Emily was crying.

Not tears of a nurse who'd just met a young child once in a surgical suite, but real tears that were ripped from her heart.

Past memories of tears rocked him. Memories of not knowing what to do. Of being helpless to ease her tears.

He wrapped his arm around her shoulders and pulled her closer, hugging her in an embrace he hoped would comfort.

Her tears worsened and Lucas felt lost.

Hadn't her tears always left him feeling lost?

Who would have dreamed that Emily would someday be sitting in a church with Lucas attending a funeral service for a child?

Not her.

She'd known today was going to be difficult, but she'd not felt right about not attending after she'd said she would. She'd braced herself. But she'd not been prepared for the onslaught of tears that had hit her as she listened to the pastor extol the boy's life and how blessed his parents had been to have him for four years.

Anger flared inside her at the man beside her for not loving her enough to want her to stay. Anger at fate that the baby she'd loved and wanted had been snatched away, too.

Anger mixed with grief so intense she thought she might shrivel up and die.

She wanted out of the church.

Lucas hugged her to him.

She didn't want his hug. Didn't want his comfort.

"Do you want to leave?" he whispered close to her ear.

She shook her head.

Not that she didn't want to leave. She did. Just that she wasn't sure her legs would hold her. If she collapsed to the floor, that would cause a scene at the boy's funeral. She wasn't willing to risk that.

"Emily?" Lucas whispered, obviously not understanding. He couldn't understand. Guilt hit her. But why feel guilty? There had been nothing to be gained by telling him. Knowing would have only possibly hurt him, too. Despite all her pain, she hadn't wanted Lucas to hurt.

She'd kept the pain all to herself.

Shaking her head, she held up her hand, silencing him.

His expression was worried. His arm tightened around her body.

The glass house Emily had been living inside for the past five years cracked, then shattered all around her as grief she'd kept buried burst free and let loose an explosion of emotions.

* * *

The funeral service ended and Lucas let out a sigh of relief. Had he known how upset attending was going to make Emily, he'd never have asked her to go with him.

He felt horrible that he'd subjected her to the funeral and helpless as she'd silently sobbed.

Had she never been to a funeral before? Perhaps not. He'd only been to a handful. His grandparents. A few family friends. A few patients. None had ever affected him the way Emily mourned for a child she hadn't known. Maybe that said something about the way he viewed life, viewed death. Or maybe it was more a sign of how she viewed those things. Emily had a big heart, always had.

"Excuse me," she said. She stood and made her way out of the chapel without a backward glance.

Watching her go, Lucas still battled confusion. Losing a patient was hard, especially such a senseless death as the young boy's had been. At least the hit-and-run taxi driver had been caught and arrested.

No matter how he tried, Lucas couldn't understand Emily's quiet sobs. He'd spent most of the service trying to figure out why she was so upset, but kept coming up with more questions.

Then again, he'd never understood her tears.

That she was gone from outside the church entrance didn't surprise him.

She'd told him to leave her alone, and he would. But he needed to make sure she was okay from the emotional beating she'd endured during the funeral.

His heart ached. How was he supposed to ignore how her body had silently shaken with tears? How was he supposed to walk away with that having been the last time he'd touched her?

He needed to tell her how he felt. Even if it was only for

her to laugh and reject him and tell him to leave, he owed it to Emily and to himself to tell her everything.

That was when he saw her, standing several hundred yards down the street. Apparently, she'd taken off walking, then decided to wait on a taxi when she'd recalled how far away they were from her apartment.

Even from the distance, he could tell she still cried.

He flagged down a taxi, got inside and then had the driver pull over to pick up Emily.

She got inside and pulled the door closed.

Lucas told the driver the address to Emily's place. She glanced up at him, obviously startled to see him inside the cab. Had she been so upset that she hadn't realized he was there?

She swiped at the tears running down her cheeks. "How do you just show up wherever I do?"

"This time it was intentional," he admitted. "I had the driver pull over to pick you up."

She turned away from him and pretended to stare out the window, but he suspected she really did so to hide her tearstained face.

"I'm taking you home, Emily," he told her, keeping his voice gentle but firm. "Then you and I are going to talk. I'm going to tell you a few things I've discovered about me, you, and about us. You're going to tell me what upset you so much at that funeral. When we're through talking, I'll leave and I'll turn my notice in at Children's, if that's what you want. For that matter, I'll leave Manhattan if you think the city isn't big enough for the both of us. But prior to my stepping out of your life forever, we are going to talk."

Lucas was so wrong if he thought Emily was going to tell him why she'd started bawling and hadn't been able to quit.

So very wrong.

What would be the point of telling him after all this time?

There was nothing he could do to change the past. Nothing good could come out of telling him. Only more pain.

Pain she already lived with.

Pain she wasn't even sure he'd feel.

Or that she hadn't believed he would feel for so many years. Now she wasn't so sure.

Having seen him with Cassie, Jenny, with his other patients, she had to question what she'd always believed. Over the years, she'd convinced herself that Lucas would have been glad their baby had died. It was how she'd dealt with the loss of him and their child.

Sitting next to him in that church, listening to that boy's funeral, that conviction had been buried.

Lucas wouldn't have wanted their baby to die.

That she'd ever believed so to begin with had been hormones and perhaps a coping mechanism to deal with her grief over losing her husband and her baby so closely together.

She'd needed him at the last funeral service she'd attended. He should have been there, but hadn't.

Despite her grief, she recognized he couldn't have been there even if he'd wanted, because he hadn't known about the small service only three guests had attended. Emily and her parents.

She choked back more tears at the memories, at the overwhelming sense of loss. "I was pregnant."

Dear God, had she really just said that out loud in the back of a taxi two blocks from her apartment? Talk about inappropriate. Talk about bad timing.

Lucas's face went ashen. "I didn't hear you, Emily."

Now was her chance. Just tell him it was nothing. That she hadn't even spoken. That what he thought he'd heard, then dismissed as having been wrong, had indeed been incorrect.

"I was pregnant," she repeated a little louder than her

first whispered admission. She turned away from him, unable to bear his confused expression, and stared blankly out the taxi window.

What was wrong with her? She couldn't stop crying and now she couldn't stop saying things she shouldn't be saying.

She didn't need to be looking at Lucas to feel his tension, to know that his entire body had stiffened.

"When?" If she hadn't known who was sitting in the back of the taxi next to her, she wouldn't have recognized his voice. He sounded distant, removed, like a stranger.

He was a stranger. Five years ago, he'd told her to leave, she had, and then he'd divorced her. Five years in which they'd had no contact whatsoever. Just because he'd jumped back into her life and into her bed didn't mean a thing.

Not a thing.

Except that once again she was crying.

She turned, met his gaze and spoke low but clearly. "When you told me the very last thing you wanted was for me to have your baby."

Lucas stared into Emily's tear-streaked, puffy face.

She'd been pregnant.

His baby had been growing inside her.

He'd told her he didn't want her to have his baby.

She'd already been pregnant.

Understanding of so much from the past hit him. Understanding of her silent sobs at the funeral.

She'd been pregnant, but there was no baby.

His insides crumbled. "What happened to our baby?"

Emily's face paled to a ghostly white. Her mouth dropped open, but she didn't speak. Her face contorted in pain and guilt hit him that he asked, yet he had to know.

"I'm sorry." He felt as if that was all he said where Emily was concerned. *I'm sorry. I'm sorry. I'm sorry.*

He was sorry.

So very sorry.

"I didn't know you were pregnant, Emily."

"I know." Her voice was a broken sob and she reached for the taxi's door handle, no doubt preparing to jump out the moment the taxi stopped outside her upcoming apartment building.

Lucas reached in his pocket, pulled out a twenty and tossed it up to the driver through the window as he followed Emily out of the car.

She went inside the building and he followed her, unable to leave, but not sure he had any right to be there.

Yes, he did have a right.

She'd been pregnant with his baby. He deserved to know more, to know the details of what had happened to their child.

Without a word, they rode up the elevator together, then she unlocked her apartment door and he followed her inside.

She tossed her over-the-shoulder handbag onto her sofa, then turned to face him. Tears streaked down her face still, gutting him. How many tears had he caused her to shed?

"Tell me what happened."

She shook her head. "It was a long time ago. I never should have said anything. You don't need to know."

For the first time a spark of anger hit him. She'd been pregnant with his baby and hadn't told him. Now she was telling him he didn't need to know about their child because it had been a long time ago?

"I'm not leaving until you tell me." His voice broke as he spoke. How did he convey that he felt grief over the loss of a child he hadn't even known about until minutes before? That he felt grief that she'd dealt with that loss by herself when he should have been there. "You should have told me years ago."

"Why?"

"Because I deserved to know." Had he really? He wasn't

sure. But he should have known. He should have been able
to look at her, his wife, and have known his baby was growing inside of her.

"How did it happen?"

Her eyes narrowed defensively. "I didn't get pregnant on
purpose, if that's what you're asking. I know that's what
your parents would have thought if they'd known, but we
always used protection. Always."

She'd talked about having a baby so often, hadn't he worried that was what she'd do? Hadn't he quit coming home
for fear that she'd purposely get pregnant? Instead, she'd
already been pregnant and had wanted him to show some
sign that he might be happy about the news. He never had,
and she hadn't told him that it was already a done deal.

Was that why she'd cried all the time? He'd thought her
depressed. Had she really been suffering from extreme
pregnancy hormone mood changes?

His short spark of anger dissipated. "I meant, how did
our baby die?"

She paced across the room, paused, her back to him. "I
started bleeding and it wouldn't stop. The obstetrician at
the emergency room said my hormones were really out of
line, that it had only been a matter of time before I miscarried as my body was rejecting the pregnancy. There was
nothing they could do."

"How far along were you?"

"Five months."

Lucas's feet went out from under him and he sank onto
the sofa. Five months. His wife had been five months pregnant and he hadn't known.

Five months. How was that even possible?

Sure, he'd stopped having sex with her for fear she'd get
pregnant, but shouldn't he have noticed something different? Or had he been so busy trying not to look at her that
he'd failed to see the obvious?

"I didn't know."

"I never thought you did. Although I could see the difference in my belly, I hadn't gained any weight overall. When dressed, it was easy to hide."

Why hadn't she gained weight? Perhaps the stress of a strained marriage? Perhaps all the tears she'd cried?

"I'm sorry, Emily." There he went apologizing again. "I should have been there."

She didn't correct him. Nor should she. He should have been by her side in that emergency room.

"Were you alone when it happened?"

"I went to my parents after I moved out of our apartment." She shook her head. "I'd felt bad all week but thought it was from what was going on between you and me. When I started gushing blood, my mother called the ambulance. She stayed with me."

"She probably hates me."

"You're not her favorite person."

"I imagine not." He tried to let it sink in. Had Emily not miscarried, he'd be a father. He'd have a five-year-old kid. Would she have told him if she hadn't miscarried?

"I had to threaten my mother that I'd never speak to her again to keep her from going to give you a piece of her mind."

"I wish she had." Because then he would have known.

Then what? What would he have done differently? Would he have gone to Emily and comforted her?

"The last thing I wanted was more drama."

Which explained why she'd just accepted his ridiculous divorce papers that he'd expected her to show up at their apartment and throw back in his face. Despite her depression, he'd expected her to fight for their marriage, to fight for him. When she hadn't and he'd realized she wasn't going to, he'd felt a devastation unlike any he'd ever known. Pride had helped him replace hurt with anger.

As with much of their marriage, he'd reacted on hot emotion when he'd filed for divorce, but, as stupid as he'd been, he'd never expected their marriage to end. He'd thought receiving the divorce papers would send Emily home, would snap her out of whatever was bothering her, would cause her to admit she had a problem and needed help. Instead, she'd signed the papers, rid her life of him and never looked back. She'd not wanted anything else from him. She'd just wanted to forget he'd ever been a part of her life and she'd moved on as if he'd never existed in her world.

He'd been the one with a problem, the one who'd needed help.

She'd given birth to a five-month-old baby.

"Did we have a son or a daughter?"

She hesitated and for a moment he wondered if she was going to tell him anything more, but then she sighed and looked so gutted his insides twisted.

"A daughter."

He'd had a daughter. A daughter whom he'd never gotten to see or hold or even fantasize about.

"They wouldn't let me see her," Emily said, her tortured words invading his thoughts, making him ache with the pain he heard in her voice.

"I wanted to," she continued. "I wanted to hold her, but they wouldn't let me."

Lucas got off the sofa, went to Emily and wrapped his arms around her while she cried. He shed tears of his own.

"You're a much better person than I am," he told her long minutes later.

Not speaking, she shook her head. "I've held that in for so long. I can't believe I told you."

"You should have told me long ago."

"Why? What good can come out of you knowing? Nothing."

"At least now I understand why you signed the divorce papers."

"You told me to leave, then sent me divorce papers. Did you think I wouldn't sign them?"

"In the middle of an argument, I told you that if you were that unhappy being married to me, you should leave. You left."

She closed her eyes. "How could I stay when you wanted me to leave?"

"I never wanted you to leave." He disentangled himself from where he held her. He needed to process the things that had happened, the things he'd learned and how he felt about those things, how he felt about Emily, about himself, about the fact he'd had a child he never knew about. "I just couldn't be what you needed me to be at that point in my life. You were crying all the time, so moody, I felt I could never do anything right, could never make you happy. Between my fellowship, my mom's grief over my grandmother's death, the financial constraints you insisted upon, the stress of wanting to be a good husband, I just wasn't coping well. When, between crying bouts, you started talking about wanting a baby, I choked. I already felt like a failure. How was I supposed to add in daddy duties?"

"I guess it's a good thing you never had to."

"No, Emily, that isn't a good thing. Not at all. Had you been upfront and told me you were pregnant, I would have wanted our baby."

"How could I have told you I was pregnant? Your parents were already accusing me of being a gold digger, warning you that I'd get pregnant on purpose. You were drifting further and further away from me and the more I tried to pull you back, the further away you slipped."

"I wasn't slipping away, Emily. I was staying away because I didn't want to make you pregnant."

She stared at him. "What do you mean?"

"I was afraid you'd intentionally get pregnant."

"I'd never have done that."

"I know that. Now. At the time, I was stressed and was hearing from all sides how I'd rushed into marriage and how you'd be quick to want to start a family so you'd have a permanent tie to my family's wealth."

"I never wanted money from you."

"No, you never did." He raked his fingers through his hair. "I'm sorry, Emily. For making you so sad, for everything I ever did wrong."

"Me, too."

Lucas wasn't sure how long he stood at Emily's window, staring down at the street below. When he turned, she sat on the sofa, watching him with her red-rimmed eyes.

He'd done that. He'd put that deep hurt inside her. He'd pushed her away and she'd lost his baby. No wonder she'd changed hospitals to get away from him. No wonder she'd not wanted anything to do with him when he'd first shown up at Children's.

He'd hurt her in ways that couldn't be easily forgotten, couldn't readily be moved beyond. The fact that she hadn't told him she was pregnant, that she'd kept something so significant from him during their marriage, caused pain he'd not easily forget or move beyond, either.

Tonight, he needed to hurt, though, to feel the pain and let it cut at his very soul while he came to grips with the past, with the loss of a baby daughter he'd not even known about.

Emily had said too much had happened for them to ever have a second chance. He hadn't understood that before.

Now he did.

# CHAPTER FIFTEEN

EMILY POKED HER HEAD into her patient's room. Her heart swelled at what she saw.

Cassie Bellows awake and, although still groggy and sleeping more often than not, holding her mother's hand.

"How's she doing this morning?"

Cassie's mother smiled. "She woke up several times during the night but seems a little stronger each time she wakes up."

"That's what the night nurse told me during report. She said Cassie was doing great."

The girl's mother nodded. "Dr. Cain says everything went as perfectly as it possibly could have when he removed the tumor. Now we just have to wait and see how successful the surgery really was or wasn't."

Dr. Cain. A man Emily hadn't seen for three days.

Three days in which he'd just disappeared from her life.

But not life in general because he'd been at the hospital each day, had done his rounds, had transferred Jenny, who was steadily improving, to the orthopedic surgical floor for further correction of her limb injuries. He'd scheduled Cassie for surgery and performed the surgical excision of her tumor early the day before.

Cassie had done great. Emily had checked on the child before she'd gone home from her shift but had made sure to carefully avoid Lucas.

If he didn't want to see her, she wouldn't put herself in his path. Not intentionally.

She didn't fool herself that she'd be able to avoid him altogether, not with them working at the same hospital. She'd toyed with updating her résumé but had nixed the idea. She loved her job at Children's and wasn't leaving. If her being there made him uncomfortable, he could leave. He'd said he would if that was what she wanted. Was it? No, she wanted him to have the opportunity to pursue his dreams, to do his research. Children's provided him with that opportunity.

They were both better off without each other.

If only she could convince herself of that.

She had five years ago. She'd convinced herself that he was a horrible person who hadn't wanted her or their baby.

That belief had been a balm for her pain and helped her move forward.

This time she knew better. She knew that her pregnancy hormones had prevented rational thought, that she'd blamed him for things that had perhaps been as much her fault as his.

Lucas was a good man, a good doctor. They'd both been immature and had made mistakes then and now.

Not that telling him about their baby was a mistake. The mistake had been not telling him immediately when she started suspecting she might be pregnant all those years ago, letting her hormones, and fear of what others thought, of what he might think, drive her thoughts to irrational limits.

But he'd already started acting so distant and somehow she'd known he wouldn't be happy with her news even before she'd started hinting about a baby. Still, she should have told him.

"Her vitals are looking really good," she told Mrs. Bellows, knowing the woman was waiting for a response of some type.

The woman nodded. Emily checked Cassie's reflexes, pleased when each one responded appropriately.

"Her neuro check is right on target."

Cassie's eyes tracked everything Emily did as she quickly assessed her patient. That the girl's eyes didn't leave hers was a great sign.

By the time Emily finished her examination, Cassie had dozed back off.

Mrs. Bellows bent over the bed to kiss Cassie's cheek. "Dr. Cain said he'd wean her off the ventilator today if she continued to hold her own."

Dr. Cain. Dr. Cain. Dr. Cain. Maybe Emily would have to rethink the whole staying at Children's thing. Listening to his patients and their families extol his virtues didn't rank high on her list of things to do if she wanted to keep her sanity.

Not that she didn't understand Mrs. Bellows's admiration of Lucas. Emily did. He'd saved Cassie's life when he'd stopped the bleed and he'd given them hope that Cassie was going to be okay when he'd removed the brain tumor.

"She is. I bet he'll be by this morning and give the order for the ventilator to be discontinued. My guess is that he only left it in overnight as an extra precaution."

The woman nodded, then glanced down at where her hand was laced with Cassie's.

"She squeezes my hand in response to my questions," the woman assured her, sounding ecstatic by the simple communication.

Emily smiled. A mother's love was a beautiful thing. Something she'd never allowed herself to really embrace. Not before telling Lucas about their baby. She had been a mother. She had loved her baby.

Telling Lucas about their daughter had healed areas of her heart she'd thought incurable.

"I asked if she knew who I was and she gave me the funniest look and tried to nod her head, then squeezed my hand. I asked her to squeeze it twice if she knew." Mrs. Bellows's voice choked up. "She squeezed it twice."

Feeling a little choked up herself, Emily patted where mother's and daughter's hands were linked. "She knows you."

Emily was sure the child did. She'd seen the recognition and love in Cassie's eyes when she'd looked at her mother.

"She really didn't wake up much yesterday but has been awake several times during the night and this morning. She never lasts long, but each time I see her eyes, it's enough to reassure me that my baby girl is still in there. But we won't really know much until the ventilator is out and we see how she responds to simple tasks."

Emily knew that it was possible Cassie would have reverted to the skill levels of a much younger child from the trauma of having part of her brain excised. Or that she might have suffered permanent damage and lost ability to stand, or walk, or talk, or so many things.

But so far every indication was that the girl's surgery had been a huge success. Emily prayed that trend continued.

"I'll be in and out checking on her, but if you need anything, don't hesitate to call me to her room."

Emily turned to leave the room and found Lucas standing in the doorway. She wasn't sure how long he'd been watching her and Cassie's mother. She supposed it didn't really matter.

She opened her mouth to speak, but nothing came out.

If he'd wanted to say something, the same thing must have happened, because he just stood there, staring at her as if trying to see inside her head.

Feeling a fool, she stood next to Cassie's bed as if paralyzed.

"Dr. Cain," Mrs. Bellows greeted him, her face lighting up at seeing him. "You just missed Cassie being awake."

"I'm sorry I missed her," he answered, dragging his gaze from Emily's.

Dear Lord, he looked good. So good her heart ached.

He'd been her husband, her lover, her best friend, and now…now she supposed he was her colleague and that would be the only link they maintained.

Sadness filled her, but she wouldn't cry.

No, she'd focus on what she had shared with Lucas, celebrate the good, put the bad behind her and move forward with her life.

She could do this.

But at the moment, she didn't feel so strong.

She excused herself from the room and left Lucas to talk with Mrs. Bellows and check Cassie.

It was what she needed to do.

She had another patient she needed to check.

She had a heart she had to start trying to piece back together. Again.

Lucas stood outside Emily's apartment door, wondering if she'd let him in.

He assumed she'd gone home at the end of her shift, but maybe not. He'd seen her talking with Meghan prior to leaving the hospital. It was possible they'd gone somewhere.

If so, then what? He'd been sitting in his office, thinking about Emily, about the past, about the present, about life. He'd kept arriving at the same conclusion. The accumulation of the past made up the present and his future, and nothing in the past, present or future mattered without Emily.

He'd headed to her apartment, not sure what he was going to do, what he was going to say, just that he had to go to her.

He didn't have time to debate within himself further because Emily opened the door and stared at him.

"What do you want?"

"You."

She grimaced. "Let's not do this. I can't handle it."

"You want me to go?" Lucas's heart pounded in his chest. Was she sending him away before he'd even gotten started spilling his heart to her?

"If you come in, we both know what will happen."

He raked his fingers through his hair. "I'm not here for sex."

"But you just said…"

"You asked me what I wanted and I told you."

The apartment door next to hers opened. A head peeked out to see who was in the hallway.

Lucas gave Emily's neighbor a reassuring smile. "Let me come in, Emily."

Emily sighed, then stepped aside. She walked over to her sofa and sat down. She picked up a throw pillow, put it in her lap and toyed with the tasseled fringe. "Sit down, please."

Lucas sat on the sofa but kept a good distance between them. He didn't want to be distracted by her nearness. He needed a clear head to tell her all the things he'd done the past couple of days.

"I checked on Cassie before I came here. She is doing great off the ventilator."

"You could have texted to tell me that," she said.

"I could have, but there's a lot more I need to tell you, Emily. Things that have nothing to do with Cassie or the hospital."

She didn't say anything, just held on to the pillow in her lap and waited.

"I've done a lot of thinking over the past couple of days," he continued. "I stayed at my parents' the other night after I left here, had breakfast with them and did a lot of talking."

"You told them about our baby? Did they think I'd gotten pregnant on purpose to try to take your money?"

Lucas sighed. "I told them. Not once did either of them say anything about you getting pregnant on purpose, Emily. They couldn't help but question you in the beginning with how quickly we met and married. There are a lot of women who marry for money."

"I didn't."

"I know that." He did know that. Maybe during prideful moments he'd let his thoughts go there, but he'd never believed Emily had married him for financial reasons. She'd loved him and had simply wanted to be his life partner. "My mother was devastated by the news you'd been pregnant and miscarried, that she may have played a role in you feeling you couldn't tell me. She wanted me to tell you how very sorry she is that the two of you never got close, that she wasn't there when you lost our baby."

A sob broke free from Emily and she swiped her eyes, covered her mouth as she whispered, "I'm sorry."

"You have no reason to be sorry, Emily. You didn't do anything wrong. My mother knows that. I know that."

"That's not true. I did a lot of things wrong. I—"

"Emily," he interrupted. "I need to finish telling you this while I can."

She folded her shaking hands over the pillow. "Okay."

"I wasn't scheduled with patients that morning, so after I left my parents, I went to your parents."

Her head jerked around to him. "You went to my parents?" she gasped. "Why?"

How could he not have?

"I needed to talk to them."

"About?"

"You. Me. Them. Our baby. Our marriage. Your depression. Everything."

"And?"

"And I'm sorry I never took the time to know your parents when we were married. They are good people."

Emily visually searched him over, possibly looking for battle wounds. There weren't any. At first he'd thought perhaps there would be, but Emily's parents had sat on their sofa, sour expressions in place, and listened to what he'd had to say.

When he'd left, Emily's father had shaken his hand, and her mother had reluctantly given him a hug. He could only hope this conversation went as well as that one.

"I can't believe you went to my parents' house." She didn't say because he'd never been there before. She didn't have to. He'd been too busy to go with her to her parents' during their marriage. He'd barely juggled visiting his own, he'd justified to himself at the time.

"Why did you go there, Lucas?"

"Because there's no way for the air to be cleared between you and me without clearing the air with them."

Her forehead wrinkled. "Why does any of this matter now?"

"It matters a great deal."

She stared at him with confusion and devastation burning in her green eyes. "I don't understand."

No, he supposed she didn't. Neither had her parents. Not until he'd told them how he'd never gotten over Emily, had never stopped caring for her, that he hadn't understood her depression, that he hoped to win her heart back, and wanted their blessing, that this time around he hoped to do things right. He'd told them he realized he didn't deserve forgiveness or second chances, but he prayed they'd give them anyway, that he prayed Emily would see beyond the past and see the man he was now, the man who had learned so many life lessons. He was sure there were many more he'd learn over the years, but he wanted Emily by his side as he faced each of those challenges.

He'd told her parents all that and more. Had told his parents that. Now he'd tell the only woman who'd ever stolen his heart.

"I love you, Emily."

Emily's ears roared and her throat thickened to where breathing felt impossible. "What did you say?"

"I love you. I always have. I always will."

Tears prickled her eyes. Why was he telling her this now? Why had he gone to her parents? Why was her heart swelling to where she thought it might burst free from her rib cage?

"I love you, too, Lucas." She always had, always would. Once she'd told him the truth, her anger at him had eased, had given way to so much more, to the truth. She loved Lucas.

She'd just never expected him to feel the same.

He moved next to her, tossed her pillow to the side and took her hand into his.

She trembled. Her hands. Her body. Her very being.

"I want to be a part of your life, Emily. I knew it after I took the job at Children's and saw you again. I just didn't understand the reasons why it was so important I be near you."

Lucas wanted to be a part of her life. Wasn't that what he'd been the past few weeks?

"I couldn't stop thinking about you, dreaming about you," he continued. "I wanted a second chance with you."

Her hand still trembled within his, but she didn't pull it away. His was trembling, too.

"I messed up when we got married, Emily. I was immature, selfish, stressed with school, stressed by my grandmother's death and how my mother wasn't dealing with that. I was distracted by life, and I lost the most important thing that's ever been mine."

She just stared at him blankly.

"You."

"You never owned me."

"Sure I did. You gave yourself to me, just as I gave myself to you. Unfortunately, I was a fool who didn't see what a prize having you was. I married you for all the wrong reasons, Emily."

Her body tensed. "I wasn't pregnant when we got married."

"No, I didn't think you were and that wasn't what I meant. I married you for my convenience."

Emily didn't understand. She gazed at him in confusion, waiting for him to elaborate.

"I wanted to have you with me when it was convenient for me. I wanted to have all my old life, but to have you there when I wanted you there. I was an idiot who didn't deserve you. I probably still don't, but I want to be a part of your life all the same."

Emily digested what he'd said. Their marriage hadn't just fallen apart because of mistakes he'd made. She'd made plenty of them, too. She'd been so intimidated by his family, so hurt by their thoughts that she'd only become involved with Lucas because of money, that she'd automatically bristled at anything to do with them or money. She'd reacted similarly to his friends. She'd isolated herself from his life outside their apartment. And then, when she'd gotten pregnant, her mood swings had gotten bad, her paranoia over her lack of fitting in had grown, her ability to rationally think things through where he was concerned had failed.

"The one thing I got right, Emily, was you. I love you. I have from the beginning. That never changed. Not through the tears I never understood. Not through the fights. Not through the divorce that never should have taken place. Not through the years that have passed." He squeezed her hand. "I resented the power you held over me."

Ha. She'd been a leaf floating in the wind, at mercy to drift whichever direction he blew.

"I was powerless."

"You may not have known it, but you had all the power where I was concerned. Stop and think about it. I abided by your rules, Emily. You said we had to live in your tiny apartment, so we did. You said I couldn't use my trust fund, so I didn't. I had a thousand demands on me from the hospital, from school, from my parents and from you. I felt as if I was going to snap. Every time we were together, all you'd do was cry, then we'd fight. The more we fought, the more I justified pulling away from you."

She pulled her hand free and scooted away from him. "You wanted to put our marriage on hold until a more convenient time?" She shook her head. "Why are you telling me this now? Any of this?"

"Because to move forward all the past has to be dealt with."

"Too much has happened for you and I to move forward."

He moved closer to her, took her hand back and gently held it within his. "I hope you don't believe that, because I don't. Not anymore."

Did she?

"I was pregnant, Lucas. I was pregnant and alone and you weren't there." She hadn't meant to say the words, wasn't even sure where they came from, but from somewhere deep, dark inside the words had leaped out, revealing her innermost pain.

"I wish I had been, Emily. If I'd known, I would have been at your side." His hand tightened around hers. "When I came home and your things were gone, I couldn't believe you'd left me. Stupid pride kicked in. I called a lawyer and set the divorce into motion. For what it's worth, I never thought we'd go through with it."

"You filed for divorce. Of course we'd go through with it."

"I thought you'd tell me where I could stick my divorce papers. It's what I wanted you to tell me."

"I got the papers on the day I came home from the hospital from losing our baby. I just looked at them and felt so defeated. I signed them and put them in the return envelope to your lawyer. My mother warned me to wait, that I wasn't thinking straight and should talk to someone before I just signed them, but I didn't have the energy to wait or fight."

"I'm sorry, Emily. I made so many mistakes, so many things I wish I could do over, but I can't. All I can do is make sure I learn from the past and never make those same mistakes again."

"I'm sorry I was so adamant about not using your trust." She bit the inside of her lip. "I was intimidated by your money. I thought if you lived within my world, we'd be okay, but that if we tried to live within yours, I'd stick out like a sore thumb and everyone would know what a fraud I was."

His eyes softened. "You weren't a fraud. You were my wife."

"I was a kid who got caught up in a love affair that she wanted to believe was a fairy tale. I realized I was too idealistic a month in. By the time I discovered our birth control had failed, I knew we'd jumped too fast."

"Emily, I don't regret having married you. I just regret our divorce."

"Me, too."

"Which brings me to why I'm here. I want to spend the rest of my life loving you, cherishing you and making up to you every stupid and wrong thing I ever did."

"No." She shook her head.

"No?"

"I don't want you trying to make up for the past. The past is done, over." Her heart ached. "I won't have you with me out of guilt."

"Woman." He pulled her to him on the sofa. "How many times do I have to say I love you before you'll understand?"

"Understand what?"

"I'm not here out of guilt. I'm here out of love. Out of a need to spend my life with the woman I want to be with above all others. The woman who I want to give everything I am to now and for forever."

He sounded like a marriage vow. The thought pinched her heart, because she knew that wasn't the case.

Could she do it?

Could she have an affair with Lucas until he tired of her and walked away?

Would he walk away?

Staring into his eyes, she wasn't so sure he would. But she didn't want just an affair. She wanted everything. She wanted to believe in fairy tales and dreams come true.

She wanted to believe in Lucas.

"I'm here to beg you to consider spending your life with me, Emily."

Was she going to refuse him? Lucas held Emily's hand within his, held his breath, prayed she felt the way he believed she felt, that too much negative hadn't happened between them to drown out all the good.

So many emotions danced across her face that he couldn't read her thoughts.

"What are you saying, Lucas?" she asked. "That you want to have an affair with me?"

An affair. He'd poured his heart out to her and she thought he was asking for sex still?

"If that's all you're willing to give me, then, yes, I'll take an affair. A lifelong one."

She stared at him, caution and the beginnings of hope in her eyes. Hope he planned to nurture for the rest of her life.

"What is it you want me to give?"

Her question was an easy one for him to answer. One he could answer with all certainty and the knowledge that Emily was his soul mate, the other half of him, the woman he wanted to wake up next to and go to sleep next to, to have her belly swollen with his children, to grow old next to, to look back on their life together and know that each step along the way had served a purpose, to teach them what was important, what was worth fighting for, what they should hold on to with all their might and hearts.

"You," he answered with his heart shining in his eyes. "Forever."

"I already did that," she reminded him, causing his heart to skip a beat. "You've always had me, Lucas. My heart, my body, all of me."

"Emily…"

"I love you, Lucas. I never stopped."

He kissed her, hard and on the mouth. "I don't deserve you."

"If this is going to work, then we have to forgive each other. Which means you do deserve me. You are a wonderful man. A wonderful doctor. A wonderful lover. A wonderful friend."

"I'd like to be a wonderful husband and father, Emily."

Emily couldn't believe her ears. "You want to get married again?"

He gave a low, nervous laugh. "This isn't how I had this part planned."

"What part planned?"

"I came here to convince you that I loved you and wanted us to be together. To talk about your depression and what went wrong between us. I'd hoped with time you'd learn to trust in our love, in us, and then I planned to propose."

Eyes wide, heart pounding, she stared at him. "You did?"

Smiling, he nodded. "I was going to take you up in the

Statue of Liberty, get down on my knee and ask you to be my lady forever."

"I'm not sure if that's the sweetest thing I've ever heard or the corniest."

"I did have a plan B if that didn't work."

"What was that?"

"I was going to whisk you off to Paris and ask you at the Eiffel Tower. If that didn't work, I'd come up with a plan C."

"Seriously?"

He nodded.

"So, really there's no incentive for me to agree."

"Only that you'd get to put this back on my finger." He reached into his pocket and pulled out a golden band.

Emily's breath caught. "You really want to get married again?"

"I do, and this time I want to do it right."

"Right?"

"I want you to walk down an aisle to me with our parents and friends there. I want to take you on a honeymoon to wherever you want to go—"

"Even if I said Atlantic City?"

His eyes glimmering, he nodded. "Even if you said Atlantic City."

"I don't need fancy weddings or fancy trips, Lucas."

His smile told her all she needed to know. He lifted her hand to his mouth and kissed her fingertips.

"Just fancy orgasms?"

"That and a fancy pediatric neurosurgeon husband. I'll be the envy of all my coworkers. They think he's pretty awesome. I agree."

"You'll marry me?"

She took his wedding band out of his hand and clasped it tightly in hers, lifting it to her heart. Rather than answering him, she rose from the sofa, went to her bedroom and returned with something she held out to him.

His eyes glassy, he looked at what she held, then met her gaze as he took the rings into his hand and closed his fingers around them.

"We've wasted five years being apart. I don't want to wait a minute longer."

"I can't believe we're even thinking this," she mused.

"I can't believe we ever let each other go."

"Never again."

"Never again," he repeated, taking her hand into his and kissing her fingertips. "I know there will be ups and downs. There are in every relationship, but I'll fight for you, for us, until my dying breath, Emily."

As she stared into his eyes, all Emily's old hurts melted away and happiness took their place.

Happiness that she knew was going to last ever after this second time around.

\* \* \* \* \*

*If you enjoyed this story, check out these other great reads from Janice Lynn*

*WINTER WEDDING IN VEGAS*
*NEW YORK DOC TO BLUSHING BRIDE*
*FLIRTING WITH THE DOC OF HER DREAMS*
*AFTER THE CHRISTMAS PARTY...*

*All available now!*

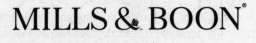

# MILLS & BOON®

MEDICAL
ROMANCE™

**THE ULTIMATE IN ROMANTIC MEDICAL DRAMA**

## A sneak peek at next month's titles...

In stores from 6th October 2016:

- **Waking Up to Dr Gorgeous** – Emily Forbes *and*
  **Swept Away by the Seductive Stranger** –
  Amy Andrews

- **One Kiss in Tokyo...** – Scarlet Wilson *and*
  **The Courage to Love Her Army Doc** – Karin Baine

- **Reawakened by the Surgeon's Touch** – Jennifer Taylo
  *and* **Second Chance with Lord Branscombe** –
  Joanna Neil

*Just can't wait?*
Buy our books online a month before they hit the shops!
**www.millsandboon.co.uk**

**Also available as eBooks.**

# MILLS & BOON®

## EXCLUSIVE EXCERPT

Luci Dawson's house-swap to Sydney starts with
a surprise when she discovers she's sleeping in a
gorgeous stranger's bed! Dr Seb Hollingsworth could
be exactly what she wants this Christmas…

*Read on for a sneak preview of*
WAKING UP TO DR GORGEOUS
*the first book in the festive new Medical duet*
**THE CHRISTMAS SWAP**

Luci was pretty sure by now that it wasn't a burglar,
but there was still a stranger in the house.

She needed to get dressed.

She switched on the bedside light and was halfway
out of bed when she heard the footsteps moving along
the passage. While she was debating her options she
saw the bedroom door handle moving.

OMG, they were coming in.

'You'd better get out of here. I've called the police,'
she yelled, not knowing what else to do.

The door handle continued to turn and a voice said,
'You've done what?'

When it became obvious that the person who
belonged to the voice was intent on entering her room
she jumped back into bed and pulled the covers up to
her chin, grabbing her phone just in case she did need
to call the cops.

'I'll scream,' she added for good measure.

But the door continued to open and a vision appeared. Luci wondered briefly if she was dreaming. Her heart was racing at a million miles an hour but now she had no clue whether it was due to nerves, fear, panic or simple lust. This intruder might just be the most gorgeous man she'd ever laid eyes on. Surely someone this gorgeous couldn't be evil?

'Don't come any closer,' she said.

He stopped and held his hands out to his sides. 'I'm not going to hurt you, but who the hell are you and what are you doing in my room?' he said.

'*Your* room?'

**THE CHRISTMAS SWAP** includes WAKING UP
TO DR GORGEOUS by Emily Forbes
and SWEPT AWAY BY THE SEDUCTIVE
STRANGER by Amy Andrews

Available October 2016

www.millsandboon.co.uk